"Do I make you nervous, Jessamine?"

"What? Of course not. What would I have to be nervous about?"

He took a step closer and she backed up. "Me, maybe?" he said. He sent her a grin that seemed positively wicked.

"N-no," she blurted out. "Not you."

"My newspaper?"

"Of course not. I'm not afraid of a little competition."

It's you I am afraid of. She cringed inwardly at the admission. She squared her shoulders and forced her eyes to meet his.

"Yeah? Then how come you're edging toward the door, Miss Lassiter?"

"I'm not!"

But she was. She couldn't get away from those laughing blue eyes fast enough.

Author Note

It is a myth that women of the Old West were solely wives and mothers. Women were as intelligent, courageous and enterprising in the 1800s as they are now, and many of them ran ranches, owned and operated dressmaking and millinery shops, hotels, boardinghouses, restaurants and saloons, and even newspapers, as this story will demonstrate. They also worked as teachers, hired housekeepers, nannies and cooks and engaged in a dozen other ventures to make their livings. In addition, women were engaged in the arts as painters, writers, lecturers and photographers, and it is to these intrepid females we owe much of our knowledge and appreciation of nineteenth-century life and culture.

LYNNA BANNING

——

PRINTER IN PETTICOATS

PAPL
DISCARDED

ISBN-13: 978-0-373-29879-2

Printer in Petticoats

Copyright © 2016 by The Woolston Family Trust

Printed in U.S.A.

www.Harlequin.com

Lynna Banning combines a lifelong love of history and literature into a satisfying career as a writer. Born in Oregon, she graduated from Scripps College and embarked on a career as an editor and technical writer and later as a high school English teacher. She enjoys hearing from her readers. You may write to her directly at PO Box 324, Felton, CA 95018, USA, email her at carowoolston@att.net or visit Lynna's website at lynnabanning.net.

Books by Lynna Banning

Harlequin Historical

One Starry Christmas
"Hark the Harried Angels"
The Wedding Cake War
The Ranger and the Redhead
Loner's Lady
Crusader's Lady
Templar Knight, Forbidden Bride
Lady Lavender
Happily Ever After in the West
"The Maverick and Miss Prim"
Smoke River Bride
The Lone Sheriff
Wild West Christmas
"Christmas in Smoke River"
Dreaming of a Western Christmas
"His Christmas Belle"
Smoke River Family
Western Spring Weddings
"The City Girl and the Rancher"
Printer in Petticoats

Visit the Author Profile page
at Harlequin.com for more titles.

For David Woolston

Chapter One

Smoke River, Oregon, 1870

Jessamine glanced up from her rolltop desk in front of the big window in her newspaper office and narrowed her eyes. What on earth…?

Across the street a team of horses hauling a rickety farm wagon rolled up in front of the empty two-story building that until a week ago housed the Smoke River Bank. A brown canvas cover swathed something big and bulky in the wagon bed.

She couldn't tear her gaze away. A tall, jean-clad man in a dusty black Stetson hauled the team to a stop and jumped down. He had a controlled, easy gait that reminded her of a big cat, powerful and confident and…untamed. His hat brim shaded his face, and his overlong dark hair brushed the collar of his sweat-stained blue work shirt.

She sniffed with disdain. His grimy clothes suggested he needed a bath and a barber, in that order. He was just another rough, uncultured rancher come to town with a load of…what? Sacks of wheat? A keg or two of beer?

The man untied the rope lashing the dirty canvas over whatever lay beneath, and she stood up and craned her neck to see better.

Oh, my father's red suspenders, what is that?

The barber, Whitey Poletti, and mercantile owner Carl Ness put down their brooms and ambled across the street to see what was going on. In two minutes, Mr. Rancher had talked them into helping him unload the bulky object. He loosened the ropes securing the thing, lowered the wagon tailgate and slid a couple of wide planks off the back end. Then he started to shove whatever it was down onto the board sidewalk.

The canvas slipped off and Jessamine gave an unladylike shriek. A huge Ramage printing press teetered on the wagon bed.

A printing press? Smoke River already had a printing press—hers! Her Adams press was the only one needed for her newspaper—the town's only newspaper.

Wasn't it?

She found herself across the street before she realized she'd even opened her office door. "Just what do you think you're doing?" she demanded.

Mr. Rancher straightened, pushed his hat back

with his thumb and pinned her with the most disturbing pair of blue eyes she'd ever seen. Smoldering came to mind. Was that a real word? Or maybe they were scandalizing? Scandalous?

"Thought it was obvious, miss. I'm unloading my printing press." He turned away, signaled to Whitey and Carl, and jockeyed the huge iron contraption onto the boardwalk.

"What for?" she blurted out.

Again those unnerving eyes bored into hers. "For printing," he said dryly.

"Oh." She cast about for something intelligent to say. "Wait!"

"What for?" he shot from the other side of the press.

"What do you intend to print?"

"A newspaper."

"Newspaper? But Smoke River already has a newspaper, the *Sentinel*."

"Yep."

"So we don't need another one."

"Nope." He stepped out from behind the press and propped both hands on his lean hips. "I've read the *Sentinel*. This town does need another newspaper."

"Well! Are you insulting my newspaper?"

"Nope. Just offering a bit of competition. A lot of competition, actually. Excuse me." He brushed past her and hefted one corner of the press. Then the three men heaved and pulled and frog-walked the bulky machine up the single step of the old bank entrance and through the doorway.

Well, my stars and little chickens, who does he think he is?

She tried to peer through the bank's dust-smeared front window, but just when she thought she saw some movement, someone taped big sheets of foolscap over the panes so she couldn't see a thing.

She waited until Carl and the barber exited and walked back across the street.

"Afternoon, Miss Jessamine," Whitey said amiably.

Her curiosity got the better of her. "What is that man doing in there?"

"Movin' in," Carl offered. "Gonna sleep upstairs, I reckon. No law against that."

Jessamine swallowed a sharp retort. She couldn't afford to insult a paying customer, even one who was at the moment helping her competition. She needed every newspaper subscriber she could get to keep her paper in the black. She had to admit that she was struggling; ever since Papa died, her whole life had been one big struggle with a capital *S*.

Carl marched past the bushel baskets of apples in front of his store and disappeared inside. The barber lingered long enough to give her a friendly grin.

"Like Carl says, no law against livin' upstairs. Specially seein' as how you're doin' the same thing."

"That man needs a haircut," she retorted. She was

so flustered it was the only thing she could think of to say.

Whitey nodded. "So do you, Miss Jessamine. Gonna catch them long curls of yours in the rollers of yer press one of these days."

Jessamine seized her dark unruly locks and shoved them back behind her shoulders. The barber was right. She just hadn't had time between setting type and soliciting subscribers and writing news stories to tend to her hair. Or anything else, she thought morosely. There weren't hours enough in the day to deal with everything that had been dropped on her.

Wearily she plodded back to her office across the street and dragged out her notepad and a stubby, tooth-marked pencil. "New printing press arrives in Smoke River," she scrawled. "Bets taken on longevity."

Cole finished cleaning the last speck of trail dust off his Ramage press, dropped the kerosene-soaked rag in the trash basket and went upstairs to unload his saddlebags. In the small bedroom he found a narrow, uncomfortable-looking cot flanked by two upended fruit crates, one of which supported an oil lamp and a grimy china washbasin. Home sweet home.

He plopped his four precious books on top of the other crate and stood staring out the multipaned window. Directly across the street he saw the *Smoke River Sentinel* office.

He'd known there was another newspaper in town; he just hadn't expected it to be located so close. Well, maybe that was a blessing. He could keep a sharp eye on the competition. Still, it was a mite more than he'd bargained for.

Was that spunky miss with all the questions the typesetter? Or the sister of the printer? Or the daughter…maybe even the wife? Pretty little thing. Rude, too. Never even introduced herself.

Well, neither had he. He must smell like a randy goat after the eighteen days he'd spent hauling that press from Kansas City. No wonder the little lady didn't introduce herself. Better rustle up a bucket or two of water for a spit bath tonight.

Tomorrow he'd stop in and make nice, but right now he was dog-tired. All he wanted was a shot of whiskey, a steak two inches thick and twenty-four hours of sleep.

Two doors down, the Golden Partridge Saloon beckoned, and next to that was the Smoke River restaurant. Handy. He swiped his hand over his stubbly chin, finger-combed his hair and set off down the street.

The whiskey was smooth, the steak rare and the bucket of water he hauled up to his living quarters was free. Couldn't beat that. He stripped, sponged off four states' worth of dirt and was just about to collapse onto the cot when he saw something out the window that stopped his breath.

Directly across from his room was another set of windows with the shades drawn. A lamp of some sort illuminated what lay behind the shades, and—good golly Molly! The silhouetted figure of a woman was moving back and forth in front of them.

A naked woman. Must be the *Sentinel* woman. Girl, he amended, assessing the slim form. High breasts, nicely flared hips, long, long hair, which she was brushing with voluptuous movements, her arms raised over her head.

Well, hell. He sure as shootin' wasn't tired anymore. He watched until the lamp went out across the way, but by then he was so aroused he was awake most of the night.

In the morning he checked the windows across the street. The blinds were up, but he couldn't see a thing with the sun hitting the glass. Just his luck. He'd have to wait for tonight.

The restaurant next door to the hotel served biscuits that just about floated off the plate and bacon so crisp it crackled when he bit into it. The plump waitress, name of Rita, was pleasant and efficient and nosy.

"New in town?"

"Yep."

"Passing through?"

"Nope. Staying."

"Don't talk much, do you?"

"Nope."

"More coffee?"

He nodded and left her a good-sized tip.

He spent the morning setting up the press, then asked around town for a typesetter. *Nada.* By suppertime he'd given up, stopped by the barbershop for a shave and a haircut and a bath, then returned to the restaurant for dinner.

"Know anyone who can set type?" he asked the attentive waitress.

"No, but I do know someone who'd like to learn," she said. She leaned toward him confidentially. "Young Noralee Ness. You'll find her at the mercantile. Her father's the owner."

"Her?"

"Sure, why not? You got something against females?"

"Not if they can set type, I don't. How come she's not working for the *Sentinel*?"

"Oh, Miss Jessamine sets her own type. Always has, even before her brother died."

Cole lowered his coffee cup. "Died?"

"That's what I said. Irate subscriber shot him."

Hell… This was no better than Kansas City. He'd narrowly escaped the same fate as a result of an editorial he'd written on abolition. Actually sometimes he wished he *had* been shot; might have been easier than what he'd gone through later.

"What was the issue?" he asked cautiously. "Not slavery, was it?"

"Nah. Election coming up. People out here get pretty riled up."

It was full dark by the time he tramped up the stairs to his quarters, and he was dead tired. But not too tired. Quickly he washed and then doused the lamp and waited.

Sure enough, about nine o'clock the blinds across the way snapped down and the light went on behind them. Cole watched until he couldn't stand it any longer, then spent the next three hours trying to get to sleep. The next morning he could hardly drag himself off his cot.

Noralee Ness turned up promptly at ten o'clock. Hell, she was only eleven or twelve years old, but her brown eyes snapped with intelligence, and she brought apples and cheese and a slab of chocolate cake for her lunch and shared it with him while he showed her how to arrange the pieces of lead type in her type stick.

She was quick to learn and even quicker with her hands. By noon he had finished the last page of the story he'd been writing, and before three in the afternoon Noralee had typeset it right down to the last comma.

Two Newspapers? Why Not?
Why shouldn't the *Smoke River Sentinel* have some competition? It's a free country. You don't have to read it if you don't want to.

Besides, the little popgun press in this town shouldn't fear a bit of healthy competition.

Or should it? Is it possible the *Smoke River Sentinel* has grown complacent because it's the one and only newspaper in this fair community?

I ask you—with an election coming up, isn't it reasonable to present two sides to every question?

Cole Sanders
Editor, *Lake County Lark*

That night before he crawled onto his cot he slipped a copy of his first edition under the door of the *Sentinel* office across the street.

Chapter Two

"Popgun press!" Jessamine screeched. "*Popgun? Just who does this Cole Sanders think he is?*"

Elijah Holst, her printer's devil, pushed his scruffy cap off his forehead with fingers stained black with ink and aimed a squirt of tobacco juice into the spittoon beside his stool.

"Fer as I kin tell, Miss Jessamine, he's the gent across the street with the fancy Ramage press."

"Gent! He's no 'gent,' Eli. He's an interloper. An opportunist. A muckraker."

"No, he ain't. He's jest another newspaper editor, same as you."

"He is not the same as me, not by a long shot. He's rude and uncouth and—"

"I hear tell he's hired the Ness girl to set type fer him."

"What? Noralee? How *could* she?"

"Beggin' yer pardon, Jess, but you cain't blame

the girl. When she wanted to come work for the *Sentinel*, you wouldn't hire her."

Cole lowered his paintbrush, climbed down from the ladder and stepped backward across the street to admire his handiwork.

Crisp black lettering marched across the doorway of the bank building he'd rented, and the name he'd carefully stenciled sent a surge of satisfaction from his brain all the way into his belly. By golly, this was better than a perfectly grilled rare steak. Better than the sight of the snow-covered Rocky Mountains. Better even than sex.

Well, maybe not better than sex. Nothing was better than holding a woman in his arms, or undressing her slowly and…

Hell and damn. He could hardly stand remembering how it had been. He'd spent long, heated nights in Maryann's arms, stroking her body and thinking he was the luckiest son of a gun on the planet.

Oh, God, remembering it felt as if something were slicing into his gut. Never again, he swore. Never, never, never again.

He refocused on the name he'd chosen for his newspaper, the *Lake County Lark*. Then he climbed back up on the ladder and added his own name in smaller printing below, followed by the word *Editor*.

This called for a shot of something to celebrate. He plopped his brush in a half bucket of turpentine and strode down the boardwalk to the Golden Partridge.

The portly redheaded bartender gave him the once-over. "New in town, huh?"

"Yeah, you might say that." He reached over the polished expanse of mahogany to offer his hand. "Cole Sanders. Just came in yesterday with my printing press and a couple bales of newsprint."

The man's rust-colored eyebrows rose. "Already got a newspaper in Smoke River, Mr. Sanders. Guess nobody told you, huh?"

"Yeah, they told me. Decided to come anyway."

"Care for a farewell drink?"

Cole laughed. "Sure. But make it a welcome-to-town shot of whiskey. I'm staying."

"It's your funeral, mister. You met Jessamine Lassiter?"

"Jessamine, huh? Works at the *Sentinel* office?"

"*Owns* the *Sentinel*." The barkeep moved away, sloshed liquor into a shot glass and slid it down to Cole. "Name's Tom O'Reilly, Mr. Sanders. I'd welcome you to town, but I figure you ain't gonna be here long."

"Care to bet on that? I just finished painting the name on my newspaper office. Paint isn't even dry yet."

Tom moved out from behind the bar, tramped over to the batwing doors and peered out. "*Lake County Lark*, is it? Kinda fancy for a small town like this."

"Maybe." Cole sipped his whiskey.

"Gotta hand it to you, Mr. Sanders. Takes nerve to run a newspaper out West."

"Not as much nerve as running a newspaper in Kansas. An *abolitionist* newspaper." He downed the rest of his drink in one gulp.

A tall gent, nattily dressed in a gray pin-striped suit and what looked like a new bowler hat, pushed through the doors and approached the bar. He nodded at O'Reilly. "The usual, Tom."

"Sure thing, Mr. Arbuckle. You met the new editor of the *Lake County Lark*?"

Arbuckle swiveled toward Cole and slapped his hat onto the bar. "Did you say newspaper editor?"

Cole nodded. "Cole Sanders," he volunteered.

"Conway Arbuckle. Next Lake County district judge. Election's in November. Can I count on your support?"

"Well, I—"

"The *Sentinel*'s backing my opponent, Jericho Silver."

"Yeah?"

"Yeah. It's really no contest, the way I see it. Me, I've got a law degree, whereas I'd swear that half-breed sheriff never got past grade school. He's figuring on 'reading law' to pass the bar exam. His wife got him a set of law books for a wedding present, see, but then she turned around and had twins last summer. Not gonna help him study law, I'm thinking."

"You married, Mr. Arbuckle?"

"Me? Nah. Never met a woman I couldn't live without, know what I mean?"

Cole signaled for another shot. No, he did not know. He'd lost the only woman he couldn't live without, but he was still breathing in and out, so he guessed he was still alive. Some days it didn't feel like it, though.

He sucked in a deep breath. "On second thought, Tom, forget the refill. Gotta get back to the office. I'm training a new typesetter."

Arbuckle frowned. "What about endorsing my candidacy, Sanders?"

Cole studied the man. Looked respectable, even with the shiny bald head under his new hat. Sounded halfway educated. Besides, a friendly rivalry between the two newspapers in town would boost his circulation. "Sure. Stop by the office tomorrow morning for an interview."

On the way down the street, he strolled past the *Sentinel* office to admire his paint job from her vantage point. Jessamine, huh? Pretty name. Starchy girl. But at least she wasn't likely to burn down his press because he backed an unpopular cause.

At the sound of Eli's scratchy voice, Jessamine dropped her gaze to the lined notepad on her desk and drew in a lungful of hot-metal-scented air.

"You gonna hurry up and finish that editorial so's I kin git to work on it?" Eli queried.

She snatched the stub of her pencil from between her teeth and crossed out her last sentence. "In a minute, Eli."

"Guess I'll eat my lunch, then." He perched on his typesetting stool and unfolded a red gingham napkin to reveal four fat cookies and a shiny red apple.

"Whatcha starin' at out the window?"

"That man across the street. He's up on a ladder doing something suspicious."

"Like what?" Eli rasped.

Jess pulled her attention away from the long legs on the fourth step of the ladder and studied instead the man's muscular shoulders and the tanned forearms that showed where he'd rolled up his shirtsleeves. "I'd give a cookie to know what he's doing over there."

"Want one of mine? Baked 'em myself. Brown sugar with raisins."

Eli boarded with widowed Ilsa Rowell. Jess paid her son, Billy, twenty-five cents each week to deliver the *Sentinel* to the town subscribers, but even with Eli paying for his room and meals, Jess knew Ilsa was having a hard time. The MacAllister boy, Teddy, took the newspaper out to the ranchers in the valley on his horse; she was happy to pay Ilsa's son to do the town deliveries.

"Whyn'tcha go on over and ask him what he's doin', Jess?"

She jerked her eyes back to the article she was composing. "Don't be silly. A good reporter learns by watching what's going on."

"And askin' questions," he reminded her.

Aha! Now the man was climbing down off his ladder, and it looked as though he had a paint bucket in his hand. He walked backward into the street, and Jess got a good look at his handiwork.

"Oh, my goodness. The *Lake County Lark*? What kind of cockamamy name is *Lark* for a newspaper?"

"Sounds kinda ladyfied, don't it?"

"It does indeed, Eli. I think we won't worry about the *Lark*. It sounds too poetic for a newspaper out here in the West. And look! There's his name underneath. Coleridge Sanders. Coleridge! No doubt he fancies himself a writer of elegant prose."

Eli crunched into his apple and Jess bent to finish the opening of her story about the new music academy in town. Maybe she'd also write an editorial about her rival newspaper in Smoke River.

Chapter Three

Jessamine waited impatiently beside the press as Eli swabbed the oily-smelling ink over the type and cranked out a proof copy. She snatched it off the press and with relish ran her gaze over her editorial.

New Editor Raises Questions
What red-blooded man would call his newspaper the *Lark*?

Is it because this editor, Mr. Sanders, intends to peck away like a bird at his competition, your long-established and well-regarded *Sentinel*?

Or is it because the man is just playing at the profession of journalism and has no intention of taking seriously the concerns of the Smoke River population?

Or could it be that the new editor, bearing the highfalutin name of Coleridge, an En-

glish Romantic poet, is just that—a romantic dreamer who lacks the manly strength to cope with the rough and ready Oregon West?
Jessamine Lassiter
Editor, *Smoke River Sentinel*

The following afternoon another issue of the *Lark* was slipped under Jessamine's door.

Whoa, Nelly!
Is the editor of the *Smoke River Sentinel* questioning the masculinity of a rival newspaper editor based on his choice of *Lark* for a name and his parents' choice of Coleridge as his given name?

While this is not libelous, it is of questionable judgment for a supposedly unbiased journalist. This editor refuses to cast aspersions on the femaleness of Miss Lassiter. However, he does question the lady's good manners. In such a personal attack I perceive a tendency toward biased news reporting. I would expect better of a good journalist.

And I also expect an apology.
Coleridge Sanders
Editor, *Lake County Lark*

That very afternoon Eli Holst marched across the street and handed Cole a copy of the latest edition of the *Sentinel*.

"Read the editorial page first," Eli hinted with a grin.

Mea Culpa...

To the editor of the *Lake County Lark*: I sincerely apologize for any inappropriate personal remarks made in the previous issue of this newspaper regarding Mr. Sanders's masculinity.

Jessamine Lassiter

Editor, the *Sentinel*

Cole settled into the chair at the corner table in the restaurant, stretched his long legs out to one side and picked up the menu. Rita bustled over, her notepad and pencil ready.

He had opened his mouth to order steak and fried potatoes when he spied someone in the opposite corner, hidden behind a copy of his afternoon edition of the *Lark*.

Well, well, well. Jessamine Lassiter. He recognized her dark green skirt bunched up under the table. Mighty flattering to find her reading *his* newspaper at supper.

Before he could stop himself he was on his feet and striding over to her table. He reached out his hand and pressed down the page of newsprint she held in front of her face until her eyes appeared.

"Interesting reading?" he inquired.

"Very interesting," she said, her voice cool. But her cheeks pinked and thick dark lashes fluttered down over her gray-green eyes.

Cole signaled Rita and reseated himself at the table next to Jessamine's. "Like I said, Rita, I'll have steak and fried potatoes."

The waitress flipped over her notepad and turned toward Jessamine. "And for you, Miss Jessamine?"

"She's having a big helping of humble pie tonight," Cole drawled. It might be the last time he'd get the best of his sharp-tongued competitor, so he figured he'd better strike while he could.

Miss Lassiter gave him a look so frosty it sent a shiver up the back of his neck, and then she raised the newspaper to hide her face.

"Chicken," came her voice from behind the page.

"Roasted or fried?" Rita asked, her voice carefully neutral.

"It was a comment, not a supper choice," Jessamine said. "On second thought, I'm no longer hungry."

Cole was on his feet before she could move, and once again he pressed down the newspaper she held aloft. "Truce, okay? You should eat supper."

"What concern is that of yours, may I ask?"

"None. Just thought it would clear the air."

She leaned forward and pinned him with a look. "Nothing will ever 'clear the air' between us, Mr. Sanders."

Cole sat down and leaned back in his chair. "How come? A war doesn't last forever. Even Bluebellies and Confederate soldiers have buried the hatchet." Ostentatiously he shook out his copy of her latest *Sentinel* edition and propped it in front of his face.

They both read in silence until Rita returned with their dinners. "Steak for you, sir." She set the sizzling platter before Cole. "And chicken for the lady."

Jessamine huffed out an exasperated breath. "I didn't order—"

"Want to trade?" Cole interrupted. He lifted away her plate of fried chicken and slid his steak platter in its place.

"Well, I—"

Rita propped both hands on her ample hips. "Oh, go on, Miss Jessamine. He's right, ya gotta eat."

Jess wanted to crawl under the dining table and bury her head in her hands. How could she have stooped to such low journalistic ethics? *How could she?*

She knew better. Her father had set a better example than that. And Miles! Her brother had lost his life defending the *Sentinel*'s policy of responsible journalism. The least she could do to honor his memory was play by the rules.

What had she been thinking?

She stole a glance at the rugged, suntanned face at the next table. It was *his* fault. That man had pushed her over the edge. His newspaper made her nervous. His presence rattled her. He had self-confidence, something she dearly wished she had more of. He was unflappable. Arrogant.

And he was laughing at her.

She couldn't stand being laughed at. Her father had laughed at her. From the time she was a baby, Ebenezer Lassiter had disparaged everything she had ever done, from making mud pies in the backyard of their Boston home to writing her first heartfelt poem to…well, just about everything she'd ever tried to do.

It was a wonder she'd grown up at all with his belittling and not withered away to a husk. If it hadn't been for her mother and her brother, Miles, she would never have survived.

Sometimes she wondered if she *had* survived. Certainly she lacked confidence in everything she'd ever tried to do, and now she found herself saddled with running a newspaper, of all things. How Papa would have laughed!

But Papa was no longer here to criticize her until she dissolved in tears. She squared her shoulders. She had not wept in over a year.

The next afternoon Jess looked up from her desk to see a figure racing past the front window, then another and another. The pounding on the boardwalk outside the *Sentinel* office sounded like thunder before a storm.

She frowned and sank her teeth into her pencil. Where was everyone going in such a rush? Then she grabbed up her notepad and bolted for the door. Her nose for news, as Miles had described it, was twitching as if it smelled something burning on a hot stove. Whatever it was, she'd break speed records to report it before Cole Sanders heard about it.

The crowd swept her along to the railroad station, where townspeople were milling about the platform. The train from the East had just pulled in. Pooh, that wasn't newsworthy unless someone important was on it. Governor Morse? General Custer? Maybe Jenny Lind? She elbowed her way to the front.

No one got off the train. Instead the engine rolled forward two car lengths to reveal the cattle car. Oh, for heaven's sake, everyone in the county had cows! There was nothing newsworthy in that unless one of them had two heads.

The crowd oohed and aahed and fell back to reveal the most beautiful horse Jess had ever laid eyes on, a handsome chocolate-colored mare. The animal stepped daintily down the loading ramp and Jess caught her breath. The horse was led by That Man. Cole Sanders.

"That's a purebred Arabian," someone yelped.

"Damn right," That Man said. He caressed the

animal's sleek head, then leaned forward and said something she couldn't hear into the creature's silky ear. She could swear the horse nodded.

"How come ya didn't ride her out here?" an elderly man shouted.

Cole looked up. "Would you hitch a thousand-dollar horse to a freight wagon?" he yelled.

"Guess not," the man admitted.

Was there a news story in this? Jess wondered. Maybe. Something glimmered at the edge of her mind, something about a man called Coleridge playing nursemaid to a horse.

She fished her pencil out of her skirt pocket, plopped onto a bench in the shade and began to scribble.

Cole watched the kid load newspapers into a saddlebag and ride out of town on his roan mare. He took his time saddling up Dancer, then cantered after the boy. Wasn't hard to catch up; the kid stopped at every ranch along the road to Gillette Springs.

Finally he trotted Dancer out in front of the roan and signaled. "Hold up, son."

The boy reined in. "Something wrong, mister?"

"Nope. Just doing a little reconnaissance, you might say." He leaned over to offer a handshake. "Name's Cole Sanders. Editor of the new paper in town."

"I'm Teddy, uh, Ted MacAllister. I'm delivering

the Wednesday edition of the *Sentinel* for Miss Jessamine."

"Mind if I ride along? I'm new to this part of the country."

"No, I don't mind."

"Might have a man-to-man discussion with you about your subscribers."

Teddy's chest visibly swelled. "Sure. Gosh, that's a fine-lookin' horse you got, mister."

"She's an Arabian. Name's Dancer. Like to ride her?"

The kid's face lit up like Christmas. "Could I? Really?"

Cole reined up and dismounted. "Sure. Let's trade for a few miles."

The boy slid off his roan so fast Cole thought his britches must be burning. He held Dancer's bridle while Teddy mounted, then hoisted himself into the roan's saddle.

"Hot-diggety, a real live Arabian!"

Cole laughed and fell in beside him. Kinda reminded him of himself at that age, young and green and working hard to hide it.

Well, he wasn't green now, and he had a score to settle. Not only had Jessamine Lassiter impugned his manhood in her editorial; she had implied he wasn't a real journalist, that he lacked both concern for Smoke River and the strength to take on the rough Oregon West.

No one, especially not a snip of a girl with a stubby pencil in her hand, said he wasn't a professional journalist.

Chapter Four

The *Sentinel* newspaper published twice a week, on Wednesday and Saturday. Cole decided the *Lark* would publish on Tuesday and Friday. That way he could scoop any breaking story and be the first to print it.

Each week he relished covering his chosen beat, the Golden Partridge Saloon, the barbershop, the potbellied stove at Carl Ness's mercantile where the townspeople and ranchers gathered to shoot the breeze and complain about whatever was stuck in their craw. And the railroad station, where each week he picked up a bundle of newspapers from the East.

The news was weeks out of date, but out here in Oregon it was still news. Custer and the Sioux, President Grant, new railroad routes. Cole discovered folks in Smoke River bellyached about everything, and that was rich pickings for a newspaper man.

The ongoing sidewalk-sweeping war between barber Whitey Poletti and the mercantile owner next door to his shop raged until the winter rains started. The dressmaker, Verena Forester, ranted at length about a lost shipment of wool bolts from Omaha. Charlie the stationmaster got so tired of sending Verena's "Where is my wool?" messages he started claiming the telegraph lines were down.

Subscriptions to the *Lark* trickled in. Cole visited every farm and rancher from here to Gillette Springs to drum up business; he even paid Teddy MacAllister an extra twenty-five cents to deliver one free copy of the *Lark* to each *Sentinel* customer on his route.

Billy Rowell, the young lad who covered the town circulation, perked right up at his offer of the same for including the *Lark* on his rounds. Jessamine Lassiter wouldn't like it one bit, but the kid confided that his pa had been killed in a mining accident last year and his momma, Ilsa Rowell, was taking in washing to make ends meet. Cole promised to increase Billy's take when the *Lark* subscriptions exceeded those of the *Sentinel*.

He pushed away from his desk and rolled his chair over to where Noralee Ness bent over her type stick. "Doing okay?"

"We're running out of *w*'s, Mr. Sanders. What should I do?"

"Improvise. Butt two *v*'s up together. Might look funny, but it'll work."

Noralee sent him a shy smile. She was proving to be a great little typesetter, quick and conscientious, even though she could only work after school and on Saturdays. She even helped Billy load up the newspapers twice each week and she never let a word slip to Jessamine about the arrangement.

He paid Noralee a dollar a week, and from the adoring look on her narrow face the first time he laid her pay envelope in her hand, he'd won a friend for life. Maybe newspapering out here in Smoke River wasn't too bad.

Except for Jessamine Lassiter. Damn woman could dig up more news from her ladies' needlework circles and afternoon teas than he could keep up with. The new music school opening next week. Births and baptisms. Weddings and funerals. The latest fashion news from *Godey's Ladies' Book,* whatever the hell that was. Even recipes for oatmeal cookies.

But the most galling was the *Sentinel'*s blatant editorials supporting Sheriff Jericho Silver for district judge. "Up by his own bootstraps" stuff. "Honest, hardworking, heroic."

Bilge. Nobody was that perfect. If he was going to support Conway Arbuckle, he'd have to dig up some dirt on Sheriff Jericho Silver.

Later. Right now he spied Jessamine sashaying across the street and into his office, where she stood in front of his desk and announced that Sheriff Silver, the paragon of Smoke River, had caught the afternoon train to Portland to take his law exam.

"You didn't know that, did you?" she taunted.

Yeah, he knew that. But when she thought she'd got the drop on him like that, her eyes snapped more green than gray, and sometimes he couldn't remember what the topic was.

"I didn't know that," he lied. He wondered if *his* eyes did anything to *her* insides, the way hers did to his. Then he caught himself and deliberately looked away. He wasn't in the market for a woman's glance. Or a woman's anything else.

"I'll scoop you on the outcome, too," she crowed. "Jericho talks only to me."

"Yeah," Cole agreed. "But his wife, Maddie, talks to *me*."

"Oh?" Her eyebrows went up. "She does? Really? When do you—?"

"When she's hanging up diapers in her backyard. Sometimes when she's out in front of her house, pruning her roses."

"Liar."

"Not. Maddie washes diapers every morning."

"And she feeds you tidbits of information every afternoon, is that it?" She puffed out her cheeks and released a long breath, making an errant curl dance across her forehead. Jessamine never wore a hat, he'd noticed. Maybe that was why she had a sprinkling of charming little freckles across her nose.

"Besides," he added, "along with some cookies and a good cup of coffee, Maddie tells me all the latest news from Pinkerton's Detective Agency in Chicago. She's an agent, you know."

"That," she said with exasperation, "is cheating."

"No, it's not, Jessamine. It's called news gathering."

She gave him a look that would fry turnips and swished out the door. He watched her skirt twitch behind her hips with every step. He couldn't wait until bedtime and another show behind her window blind.

At noon, Conway Arbuckle paid him another visit. "Say, Sanders, whaddya think about running another editorial about my superior qualifications for district judge?"

"Already ran two editorials this week." Cole noticed that every time Conway visited the *Lark* office, Noralee turned her back, keeping her head down and bending over the rack of type fonts as if they were Christmas packages.

"You got something new to say?" he queried.

"Hell yes, I do," Conway snapped. "Seems that Sneaky Pete sheriff's run off to Portland. Wonder what he does in the big city?"

"He's taking his—"

"Prob'ly a woman, wouldn't you say?"

"No, I wouldn't say, Mr. Arbuckle. Sheriff Silver's a married man with two kids. Twins."

Arbuckle leaned over Cole's desk and spoke in a low tone. "So? I smell a rat? Cant'cha dig up some dirt on him? You know, a nice-lookin' whore—"

"Watch it, Arbuckle. There's a lady present."

Arbuckle jerked upright. "Huh? Where? You mean your type girl? Hell, she's only a kid."

"She's a 'she,' no matter how old she is. Now get out and leave us in peace. When there's legitimate news about Sheriff Silver, I'll publish it."

Noralee watched the door close behind Conway Arbuckle and swiveled on her stool to turn worshipful brown eyes on Cole. "Do you think I'm really a lady, Mr. Sanders? I'm only eleven."

Cole rose. "Miss Ness, you are every inch a lady. I'll stand up for you any day. Now, what about our *W*'s? You need any more?"

"That man has bad breath," Noralee remarked. "Could you write about that?"

Cole chuckled. "Nah. Gotta have a Who, What, Where, When and Why to make a story."

But, now that he thought about it, maybe it was time in this election campaign to aim for the solar plexus.

Jessamine folded the last of her Saturday edition into Teddy MacAllister's saddlebag and handed the rest of the stack to Billy Rowell for the town deliveries, along with a shiny new quarter for each boy. She frowned as she watched Billy lope off down the street. She'd seen him in town just yesterday, hanging around the *Lark* office with an expectant look on his face.

You don't suppose…?

She most certainly *did* suppose. That snake Cole Sanders was trying to use her delivery boy! She marched out the door and across the muddy street so fast Eli sat up on his stool, his mouth hanging open.

"Mr. Sanders," she announced the instant she was inside his office.

Her nemesis stood up behind his desk. "Miss Jessamine. Beautiful afternoon, isn't it?"

"Don't change the subject," she replied sharply. "You're using Billy Rowell as a delivery boy, and I strongly object. Very strongly, in fact."

"Well, don't. Doesn't take much to get you riled up, does it?"

She ignored the remark. "Stealing my delivery boy is unconscionable."

"Unconscionable," he echoed. "Shockingly unfair. Unjust. Unscrupulous. But unconscionable? Kinda strong word for a simple matter of hiring a free agent to do a job."

Behind her she heard a spurt of laughter from Noralee Ness.

"Billy isn't a free agent," Jessamine countered. "He belongs to me."

Cole liked it when she got angry. Her cheeks turned rosy and she bit her lips until they were swollen and the color of ripe raspberries. He was finding it hard to look away from her mouth.

"On the contrary, Jessamine, Billy Rowell doesn't belong to you or anybody else in this town except maybe his momma, who, by the way, seems mighty grateful for the extra money her son's bringing home each week."

Jessamine's raspberry-bitten lips opened and then closed. And opened again. "Of course," she said in an even tone. "You are correct. I do beg your pardon for the use of 'unconscionable.' What about just 'unfair'?"

"Seems to me, Miss Jessamine, you go off half-cocked a lot."

"That, Mr. Sanders, is entirely your fault."

"For God's sake, we've been squabbling for weeks now. About time for first names, isn't it?"

Another snort of laughter from Noralee.

"Now," he continued, noticing how Jessamine's breasts were swelling against the buttons of her white shirtwaist, "what is it exactly that is my fault? Other than running my newspaper office across the street from yours?"

She actually stamped her foot on the plank floor. "For one thing, you are—"

Jess stopped midsentence. He was what? A competitor, yes. A man, with all the maddeningly masculine habits of men, a lazy, confident swagger when he walked; a slow, suggestive smile that made her insides turn mushy; a mouth that… Oh, she didn't know what, but his lips too often drew her gaze and she just knew that he noticed.

"I am…?" he prompted.

"You disregard, um, propriety. You…drink. You… are backing that snake Conway Arbuckle for judge."

"It's true, I do drink. I consider the Golden Partridge part of my news beat. But propriety? I don't disregard propriety, Jessamine. I have never—"

He broke off and swallowed hard. Yes, he had disregarded propriety. He'd swept Maryann off her feet right under the nose of her stepfather and run away with her before the old man could unearth his shotgun.

"Also," he continued, "Mr. Arbuckle asked for my support. Besides that, since I took him on, my subscriptions have increased almost twofold."

She sniffed. "That's because people sense a fight between the *Sentinel* and the *Lark* over the election." She sniffed again.

"Naturally. We both want to sell newspapers, right? Competition brings in more customers, Jessamine."

She said nothing, just chewed some more on her lips. If she didn't stop, he'd have trouble hiding his body's reaction.

Too late. He stepped sideways, out of both Jessamine's and Noralee's field of view, and surreptitiously adjusted his jeans.

"Customers," she murmured at last. "I see. Well, I suppose you are correct. I wonder why I didn't consider that before."

"Seems to me you often speak first and consider later."

That elicited a choked laugh from Noralee.

Jessamine said nothing for so long Cole thought maybe he'd gone too far. She stood motionless, studying her shoe tops and worrying her bottom lip.

Jessamine realized she was standing tongue-tied in Cole's office and couldn't for the life of her remember what she'd come for. *Think of something. Anything.*

"I...um..."

"Yes? Something else on your mind?"

"Yes, there is," she admitted. "But now I can't remember what it was."

His eyes crinkled at the corners. "Do I make you nervous, Jessamine?"

"What? Of course not. What would I have to be nervous about?"

He took a step closer and she backed up. "Me, maybe?" he said. He sent her a grin that seemed positively wicked.

"N-no," she blurted. "Not you."

"My newspaper?"

"Of course not. I'm not afraid of a little competition."

It's you I am afraid of. She cringed inwardly at the admission. There hadn't been a male since she was twelve years old who made her heart thrum in irregular beats and her words dry up on her tongue. She squared her shoulders and forced her eyes to meet his.

"I d-don't scare easily, Mr. Sanders." She thought he looked just a tad disappointed.

"You don't," he stated. His tone said he didn't believe her for one minute.

"The newspaper business out here in the West is fraught with danger. If I were going to go all jelly-legged over something I would have done so when my father died and my brother was shot and left me running the *Sentinel*. As it is, you don't scare me one whit."

"Yeah? Then how come you're edging toward the door, Miss Lassiter?"

"I'm not!"

But she was. She couldn't get away from those laughing blue eyes fast enough. She whirled toward the door and ran smack into Ellie Johnson, the federal marshal's wife.

Ellie reached out to steady her. "Jessamine?"

"Ellie! I was just leaving. Please excuse me."

She fled through the open door and didn't stop until she was all the way across the street.

Cole watched her disappear through the *Sentinel* office doorway. "Don't know what got into her," he murmured.

"Maybe she's hungry," Ellie offered with a laugh.

"Nah, she just finished breakfast."

Ellie nodded. She was as tall as he was, with a slim figure and a graceful way of moving. He thought he recognized her from her photo in the *Sentinel*.

"Mrs. Johnson, isn't it?"

"Ellie."

Cole nodded. "What can I do for you today, Ellie?"

She smiled. "It's about what I can do for *you*, Mr. Sanders."

Cole waited while her smile widened. "Uh, what might that be? You aren't a typesetter, are you?"

Behind him, Noralee gave a squeak of outrage.

"Heaven's no. I'm a music teacher. I came about tonight."

"Tonight? What about tonight?"

"Why, the tryouts for the choir," she explained. "At the church."

"Sorry, I'm not a churchgoing man." He hadn't set foot in a church since that awful day back in Kansas when he buried Maryann.

"Oh, it's not a church choir," she said quickly. "It's the new community chorus that I am directing. We're doing a Christmas benefit for the new music school."

"Oh, yeah?"

"Do you like music? Singing, I mean?"

"I do. But not in church."

"Whyever not? What have you got against churches?"

"I…" Cole faltered. He could never explain how he felt, that God had abandoned him to black despair when Maryann had died. He shook his head.

"Do come," she urged. "A little religion would do any newspaper editor good. Seven o'clock."

She was gone before he could say yea or nay. Mostly he thought nay. A little religion would never in a thousand years cure what ailed him.

But then he thought of all the town news he might glean at choir rehearsals, and he changed his mind.

Chapter Five

Cole hated churches. He'd been married in one and a year later he'd sat through Maryann's funeral and felt his heart turn to stone. Ever since then he'd steered clear of religious establishments.

To his surprise, the Smoke River Community Church meeting hall wasn't oppressive. The walls were painted a soft cream color, accented by dark wooden beams. Oak, he thought. Nice.

About two dozen townspeople sat on benches around the perimeter, waiting for the tryouts to begin. Including, he discovered with a jolt of pleasure, Jessamine Lassiter.

Tryouts, he discovered, involved singing alone, and Cole immediately felt uncomfortable about that. *Trapped* would be a better word. Maybe he should give up the idea. He had started to rise when the choir director, Ellie Johnson, impeccably dressed in a black skirt and a soft pink shirtwaist, clapped her hands and everyone sat up straighter.

"Let's start with the women's voices."

The women sang selections from church hymns for their tryouts. Ellie selected four altos and three sopranos that blended with each other. One of the sopranos was Jessamine, who had spent all evening studiously ignoring him.

The tenors tried out next. The director chose five, including Whitey Poletti, who had a whiskey-smooth tone and an extraordinarily high range. Whitey had launched into "Santa Lucia," but got no further than the first stanza before Ellie smiled and nodded at him.

By the time the director got around to the baritones, Cole was ready to bolt. He couldn't sing like Whitey. He had no musical training, never sang in a church or any other choir and he hated the thought of doing it in public.

He looked for the exit, but just then Ellie pinned him with an expectant look.

He maneuvered to sing last, praying that those already chosen, including Jessamine, would go on home.

No such luck.

"Cole Sanders? Your turn."

Cole stood up, wishing a trapdoor would open beneath him. The director smiled encouragingly. "What would you like to sing, Mr. Sanders?"

He felt Jessamine's cool green-gray eyes on him, and his throat closed up tight. The director waited.

"Uh, could I do this outside? Just the two of us?"

She shook her head, and the onlookers began to whisper among themselves. Shoot sake! This wasn't any worse than facing down a rabid mob of pro-slavery demonstrators back in Kansas. He drew in a deep breath.

Jessamine waited. She'd bet the country bumpkin from Kansas couldn't sing a note. Then he opened his mouth and started in.

"'Oh, my darling, Oh, my darling, Oh, my darling, Clementine…'"

Suddenly the room was so quiet she could have heard a hatpin hit the floor. She sat straight as a ramrod and stared at him.

"You are lost and gone forever…"

She'd never heard a more beautiful male voice. Rich and full, like a hot mince pie warm from the oven. The director stopped him after "dreadful sorry, Clementine."

"Mr. Sanders, do you read music?"

Aha! Jess would bet a million dollars in gold that he couldn't. That was why he'd chosen a simple folk song for his audition, and besides that, his voice was entirely untrained.

"Yeah, some," he said. "My momma taught me when I learned to play the guitar."

"Then we would be honored to have you in our community choir. We'll be performing selections from Handel's *Messiah* at Christmas. Are you familiar with this work?"

Cole shook his head.

"In addition to the choral numbers, there is also a mixed quartet of voices included—soprano, alto, tenor, baritone. Perhaps you would consider—?"

"Just four voices singing by themselves? 'Fraid not, ma'am. I—"

The director stepped up close to him. "Please, Mr. Sanders. I am short one good baritone voice."

Jessamine clenched her fingers together in her lap. *Say no,* she urged. Ellie had chosen her to be the soprano singer in the quartet. The last thing she wanted was to stand next to Cole Sanders and sing. The very last thing. The thought made her cold and then hot all over.

She caught Cole's eye and subtly shook her head.

He gave her a long, unreadable look. "I'll do it," he announced.

Jess's heart contracted. She sat numb with anxiety while Ellie selected two basses, rancher Peter Jensen and Ike Bruhn, who owned the sawmill.

"That will be all for tonight," Ellie announced. "Rehearsals will start next Tuesday when Winifred Dougherty's grand piano arrives from St. Louis. Until then, pick up a score and look it over." She gestured to a pile of music on one of the benches.

"And for the quartet…" She glanced meaningfully at Cole and then Jessamine. "Please start learning your parts. We will rehearse separately, on Thursday evenings."

Jess pressed her lips together. It wasn't enough to

have Cole Sanders in her hair every day of the week, but nights, too? She considered dropping out of the choir, but she'd looked forward to singing the *Messiah* ever since Ellie had chosen it.

She would just have to cope. She'd lived through worse than standing next to Cole Sanders. When Miles was killed she'd wanted to give up on life, but she hadn't. Now singing was something that kept her alive inside. She prayed she could manage to learn her part. Even when she was a child, her father said when she sang she sounded like a sick cat.

Cole made a move toward her, but she slipped out the side door. She was still trembling inside at the prospect of standing next to him twice each week. She comforted herself with the knowledge that it would only be until Christmas.

But Christmas was weeks and weeks away. Oh, bother. She would just have to learn how to keep the man from nettling her at close range.

Cole stared down at the draft page of his latest editorial, scattered across his desk. Time to pull out all the stops, he guessed. He hated to ride Jessamine any harder, but newspapering was a business like any other.

He dipped his pen in the ink bottle on his desk. Let's see, now…

"Arbuckle Opponent Cowers," he wrote. Good headline.

Yeah, that ought to do it. Something to elicit a response from the *Sentinel* and bring in some more subscriptions.

"We note the recent absence of Sheriff Jericho Silver," he continued. "And we wonder. Is it possible the man is hiding from confrontation with his opponent, Conway Arbuckle?"

He ran his hand across his stubbly chin. He needed one more verbal jab to draw blood.

"Only a coward would skulk in his jail-cell office instead of getting out and campaigning among the good voters of Smoke River."

"Noralee," he called. "Set this up right away, will you?"

Tuesday night rolled around. Cole rode back into town after delivering the last of his papers to his outlying subscribers, hurriedly sponged off, ate a quick supper at the restaurant and made it to the choir rehearsal with five minutes to spare. He hoped Jessamine had read his editorial.

The new music school smelled like fresh paint and new wood and had ample seating for the twenty-seven-member chorus now drifting in for rehearsal in twos and threes. Good acoustics, too, Cole noted as their chatter reverberated around the room.

The morning rain had eased off, and outside the air smelled of frost. Felt like it, too. Women were bundled up in wool fascinators and fur muffs, and men lumbered in wearing sheepskin coats or wool mackinaws and leather gloves.

Jessamine Lassiter entered, stamping her feet and blowing on her fingers. He knew she'd already read his latest edition when she sidled past him and hissed a single word at him. "Snake."

She took a seat next to the potbellied stove in the corner and glared at him with eyes like green jade. Her nose and cheeks were reddened from the cold.

They all stood to warm up their voices, and then the director arranged them by vocal part, basses on the left, then tenors, baritones, sopranos and altos on the far right. The piano accompanist, Doc Dougherty's wife, Winifred, struck a chord.

Cole could hear Jessamine's clear, sweet soprano soar above the others, and a shiver went up the back of his neck. Anger sure made her voice sound beautiful.

Then Ellie Johnson dropped her arms. "I want to mix up the voices more, to get a better blend." Instead of standing in vocal sections, she arranged them in quartets—one soprano, one alto, a tenor and a baritone, all grouped close together.

Cole ended up standing beside Jessamine. She held herself rigid, as if her corset stays were made of iron, and he fancied he could see sparks pop off her body.

The choir la-la-la'd up and down a scale, and now he was quite sure fury was affecting her voice. Her enunciation was so crisp her tongue could cut paper, and the tone… Jehosephat, it was so clear and beautiful it stopped his breath.

"Jer-i-cho-Sil-ver-is-not-a-co-ward," she sang up and down for the next scale. She glared at him for emphasis.

He cleared his throat. "He-is-too-a-coward," he sang.

Her cheeks flushed as she attacked the next scale, this time in a minor key. "Just-you-wait-you-snake-la-la-la-la."

The rehearsal itself wasn't near as much fun as the warm-up scales and the la-la-la battle with Jess. Then the words of the *Messiah* took precedence over the insults they were passing back and forth. Cole was halfway disappointed.

But what almost did him in was standing next to her, catching the scent of her skin as the room warmed up, smelling her hair as that tangle of wild curls bobbed near his shoulder. He groaned without thinking.

Watch out, Sanders. After Maryann you swore you'd never have thoughts about another woman. Well, hell, he wasn't having *thoughts*. He was having *feelings*. Normal male feelings. Feelings of the most basic variety. Feelings of just plain wanting.

But, he assured himself, his mind was in full control. A man could *look*, couldn't he? Just as long as he didn't let Jessamine Lassiter mean anything to him beyond admiration for a pretty rival newspaper editor. Just as long as she didn't *matter* to him.

Maybe he should just crawl onto his cot tonight and forget about watching her silhouetted form against the window blind across the street.

At that moment she tossed her shiny dark hair back over her shoulders and he sucked in his breath. Or maybe not. Damn, she smelled good.

Ellie had the sopranos sing the next section by themselves. Standing next to Jessamine, Cole tried to keep his mind on the music instead of surreptitiously watching her.

"'For unto us a child is born...'"

He worked hard to screen out Jess's lilting soprano voice, but with little success. He heard every single syllable, felt every indrawn breath she took until he found himself unconsciously breathing right along with her. It was a bit like making love, he thought. Instantly he wished he hadn't thought it.

She moved unconsciously when she sang. Just enough to bring her body an inch or two closer to his. He began to sweat.

Too close.

Not close enough.

Despite the chill in the rehearsal room, his body began to grow warm. He fought an urge to rip off his flannel shirt, but he settled for rolling his sleeves up to his elbows.

Big mistake. As she swayed beside him, the hair

on his forearms rose as if reaching toward her. The urge to feel her skin brush against his was overpowering.

Move toward me, Jessamine. Touch me.

Shoot, he was going nuts. Another hour of this would make him crazier than a wolf in heat. He sidled away from her, and tried to control his hammering heartbeat.

What he couldn't control was his groin swelling into an ache. He wanted to toss her over his shoulder and take her...where?

He suppressed a groan. *To bed.*

Oh, God.

That night he didn't sleep at all.

Chapter Six

Jessamine headed across the street, her footsteps crunching against the frost-painted boardwalk; it was so slick she had to concentrate to keep her balance. Mercy, it was cold this morning! She saw no sign of life at the *Lark* office, so she bent and carefully laid the Wednesday edition of her *Sentinel* against Cole Sanders's door.

Back in her own office, she turned her backside to the potbellied stove in the corner and rubbed her frozen hands together.

"Cold out, huh, Jess?"

"You know it is, Eli. The temperature outside is below freezing."

"Gonna be a lot hotter when Sanders wakes up and reads yer editorial."

She ducked her head to hide her smile. "Cole Sanders is a grown man, Eli. Sticks and stones and so on."

"Yep, reckon so. Names ain't never hurt you, huh?"

Jess sobered instantly. Names *had* hurt her. When she was young and just starting out to help her papa and Miles on the newspaper, her schoolmates had teased her mercilessly about her ambition to be a journalist. "What d'ya wanna do that for? Too ugly to get a husband? Boys don't like brainy girls, smarty-pants!"

And it was names in an editorial her brother had printed that had cost him his life; that had hurt even worse. After Papa died, she and her older brother had moved out West and Miles had taken her under his wing.

She had been just a young girl, but he had begun teaching her about operating a newspaper, things her father had never let her do such as cleaning the ink off the rollers and setting type. Miles had also let her try her hand at writing stories, and he instructed her in the basics of journalism—being accurate and objective.

Then Miles had been killed, and now she was struggling to carry on the newspaper he had established in Smoke River.

Jess didn't really think Cole Sanders would shoot her for writing an inflammatory editorial. But she would wager he might *want* to. She bit the inside of her cheek. This morning she couldn't help wondering what the no-nonsense editor of the *Lake County Lark* would do about the editorial she'd published.

She kept one eye on the front windows of the *Lark* office across the street and set about planning her Saturday issue. She'd write a feature story about the new choir Ellie Johnson would be directing, and another article on the children's rhythm band the music school director, Winifred Dougherty, was starting, together with the director's plea for a violin teacher. Maybe she'd add an interview with the sheriff's wife, Maddie Silver; what it was like being the mother of twin boys while also a Pinkerton agent?

Across the street the front door of the *Lark* office banged open and Jess caught her breath. Then just as suddenly it slammed shut. Cole had picked up her newspaper and retreated inside. She waited, her heart pounding.

Eli held up the flask of "medicinal" whiskey he kept under the counter. "Want a snort?"

"Certainly not." She tried not to watch the front door of the *Lark* office, and then suddenly it flew open again. She gasped and held her hand out to Eli. "Well, maybe just a sip."

Cole Sanders started across the street toward her, his head down, his hands jammed into the pockets of his jeans, and a copy of her newspaper stuffed under his arm. Jess uncorked Eli's whiskey bottle and glugged down a double swallow.

Cole marched straight for her office, his face stern, his boots pounding the muddy street. Jess bit her lip, stiffened her spine and laid her hand on the doorknob. She would do her best to smile and graciously welcome him inside.

But she glimpsed his brown sheepskin jacket moving past her front window and on down the boardwalk.

The air in her lungs whooshed out. What on earth? Didn't he want to yell at her about her editorial? She'd used the word *insidious* more than once, and *nasty* at least twice. And her new favorite word, *larcenous*; she'd used that one three times. She really relished *larcenous*. She'd even put it in boldface type.

Wasn't Mr. Sanders livid with fury?

She couldn't stand the suspense. She grabbed her heavy wool coat and knitted green scarf off the hook by the door.

"Hey, Jess," Eli yelled. "Where are ya...?" She blotted out his voice and sped down the frost-slick sidewalk.

Then her steps slowed. Drat. If Cole stopped at the Golden Partridge she couldn't follow him. No lady entered a saloon.

But he strode past the Golden Partridge and entered the restaurant nearby. Thank the Lord. She could unobtrusively steal inside, sit in one corner sipping a cup of tea and watch his face while he read her editorial.

She tiptoed inside the deserted restaurant, shed her coat and scarf and hung them on the maple coat tree in the corner. "Hot tea, please, Rita," she whispered.

Cole sat with his back to her, calmly sipping a mug of steaming coffee. But he wasn't reading her newspaper. He was gazing out the front window. And humming! She recognized the tune, "The Blue-Tail Fly."

Rita brought her a ceramic pot of tea, plunked it down and tipped her gray-bunned head toward the front table. "Kinda odd, you two settin' in the same room but not havin' breakfast together."

"Oh, Mr. Sanders and I are not together."

The waitress blinked. "No? Shoot, I thought—"

"Sure we're together," Cole said without turning around.

Jess jumped. The man must have ears like a foxhound.

"You misspelled *larcenous*," he called.

"What? I thought you hadn't read my editorial yet."

He maneuvered his chair around to face her. "Oh, I've read it all right. Like I said, you misspelled—"

"I heard you the first time," she retorted.

"Never figured you for a sloppy writer, Miss Lassiter."

"I never figured you for a schoolmarm, Mr. Sanders."

"Point taken." He rose and came across the room to her table. "Scrambled eggs?"

"No, thank you. I am having tea."

"Rita, scramble up some eggs for me and the lady. Add some bacon, too."

Rita bobbed her head, hid a smile and disappeared into the kitchen.

"Cold out this morning," Cole said amiably.

"Very." Jess fiddled with her napkin, refolded it into a square, then shook it out and folded it again. "Very well, how *do* you spell *larcenous*?"

"Hell, I don't know. Got your attention, though, didn't it?"

She bit her lip. "It most certainly did. Are you always so underhanded?"

"Nope. Hardly ever, in fact."

"Only with me, is that it?"

Cole leaned across the table toward her and lowered his voice. "Jessamine, if you don't stop worrying your teeth into your lips like that, so help me I'm going to kiss you right here in front of everybody."

Her eyes rounded into two green moons. "I. Beg. Your. Pardon?"

"You heard me. Stop biting your lips."

She turned the color of strawberry jam. "What business is it of yours what I do with my lips?"

"None at all. But I'm only human, and I'm male, so stop it."

She tossed her napkin onto the table and started up, but he snaked out his hand and closed his fingers around her wrist.

"Sit." He gave a little tug and her knees gave way.

"Now," he said in a businesslike tone. "We're gonna have a council of war, Miss Lassiter, so listen up."

She opened her mouth, then closed it with a little click, and he proceeded.

"Some things are fair in journalistic jockeying, and some things are hitting below the belt. What you wrote about Conway Arbuckle is below the belt."

"What things?"

He dragged her newspaper from inside his jacket pocket, spread it flat on the table and tapped his forefinger on her editorial. "That he's larcenous. And that he's a cheat. You shouldn't sling mud around with accusations like that unless you can back them up with facts."

"What if I *can* back them up?"

"I'm betting that you can't."

"How would you know?"

"Jessamine, you keep this up and Arbuckle will sue you for everything you've got."

Her face turned whiter than the tablecloth. She studied the teapot, her spoon, the squashed napkin that lay on the table between them. At last she looked up at him, and his heart flopped into his belly.

Tears welled in her eyes. Big shiny tears that made him want to lick them off her cheeks.

"When Miles…" She bit her trembling lip and Cole stifled a groan.

"My brother was always the brainy one," she said on a shaky breath. "We came from a long line of newspaper publishers, our great-grandfather in England, and our grandfather and father in Boston. Papa taught Miles everything, and I...well, I just tagged along because I was a girl. When Papa died we came out West to start over on our own, and then...then Miles was killed and I—I am doing my best to carry on the family tradition. "

"And you're doing fine, Jessamine. But you might, uh, ask Sheriff Jericho Silver what his law books say about defamation of character. And libel."

The color drained from her face. "L-libel? Miles never talked about libel."

"That's probably what got your brother killed. Jessamine, exactly how much do you know about editing a newspaper?"

She drew herself up so stiff he thought she'd pop the buttons off her red gingham shirtwaist. "I know enough," she said in a tight voice.

"Not hardly." He tried to gentle his voice, but he was irritated. Damn fool woman. No doubt she'd stepped up to fill her brother's shoes and take on the newspaper, and he had to admire her for that, but wanting and succeeding were two different things. Doing it badly could get her killed.

"There are rules," he said. "Good journalists don't go off half-cocked, and good journalists don't sling accusations around without hard facts to back them up."

"Oh." She sounded contrite, but her eyes were blazing. "Exactly why are you helping me, Cole? After all, we are competitors."

"You're darn right, we are competitors. But look at it this way, Jess. We may be on opposite sides of the fence, but actually we're helping each other. My subscriptions have nearly doubled. I'd wager your subscriptions are up, too. But if your newspaper goes under, there goes reader interest in the competition between my *Lark* and your *Sentinel*."

She gripped the handle of her teacup so tight he thought it might snap off. "I've sunk every last penny I have in the *Sentinel*," she said in a shaky voice. "I cannot afford to fight a lawsuit."

"Then don't. Get yourself a set of law books and start studying what's libelous and what's just legitimate criticism."

She opened her mouth to reply, but Rita interrupted. "Eggs and bacon, right?" She plopped down two loaded platters and stepped back. "You two aren't gonna fight over breakfast, now, are you?"

"Not this morning," Cole said with a smile.

"I guess not," Jessamine said in a small voice. "Not when I'm this hungry."

Cole crunched up a strip of crispy bacon. "Hunger makes us good bedfellows."

She flushed scarlet and he suddenly realized

how that might have sounded, but it was too late. Then with extreme care she upended her teacup and poured the hot liquid over his knuckles.

While he mopped at his hand and swore, she calmly picked up her fork. "Bedfellows?" she said, her tone icy. "That remark is positively indecently suggestive. I should sue you."

Cole bit back a laugh. "Yeah, well, it just slipped out. But maybe you should think about it."

"Think about what?"

Bedfellows, he almost blurted. "Libel," he said instead.

She pushed away from the table and stalked out, her behind twitching enticingly.

At the choir rehearsal that evening, Cole appeared with a bandage wrapped around his hand and an odd gleam in his blue eyes. Jess smothered a stab of regret over her impulsive act at breakfast and concentrated on not biting her lips.

The director clapped her hands for attention, and the singers rose to begin their vocal warm-ups.

"You're dangerous, you know that?" he whispered when he and Jessamine stood side by side.

"And you," she murmured, "are insulting."

"I meant the word *bedfellows* figuratively speaking," he intoned.

Jessamine turned away, but she wondered at the niggle of unease that burrowed under her breastbone.

She wished, oh, how she wished, she didn't have to stand next to Cole Sanders one more minute.

It wasn't that he sang off-key. Quite the contrary. His voice was warm and, surprisingly, he read music better than either tenor Whitey Poletti or alto Ardith Buchanan. And he paid attention to Ellie's directing better than she was at the moment.

It wasn't musical unease she felt. It wasn't even unease about their competing newspapers. It was how he made her feel when she stood so close to him she could sense the sleeve of his blue wool shirt brush against her arm. She wanted to lean into his warmth, his strength. He made her feel small and fragile in a way she had never felt before.

Even as a schoolgirl, she had never hesitated to double up her fists and pound any boy who made one of her friends cry. Miles said she had been a real stoic when Mama died and then Papa had succumbed to a heart attack.

But the truth was that Cole Sanders made her feel not only fragile but both furious and frightened at the same time. Furious when he exposed how much she didn't know about running a newspaper and frightened at the hot, trembly feeling that built inside her when she stood near him.

As a dried-up spinsterish twenty-two, she was shocked by her reaction. But she was too old to force her hands into fists and beat him up for upsetting her. And Lord knew she was too young to know anything about men and what went on inside them. Cole had smiled at her, but what did that mean? The truth was that Cole Sanders kept her feeling off balance.

And no matter what he said about the advantages of their newspaper competition, she would bet he was just waiting for her to make a dire mistake so he could force her *Sentinel* out of business.

She straightened her spine. Whatever it was Cole Sanders wanted, she would never let him have it.

Chapter Seven

"Mr. Sanders?"

Cole kept his gaze on the page proof spread out on his desk. "Hmm? What is it, Noralee?"

"How do you know when you fall in love?"

"What?" His head jerked up. "What did you say?"

Noralee scuffed her leather heels against the bottom rung of her stool. "I said," she repeated, annoyance coloring her voice, "how do you know when you fall in love?"

Cole stared into his typesetter's guileless brown eyes. "Well, uh…"

"My sister, Edith, she's my twin, she says your head goes all fuzzy and your heart doesn't beat right."

"She does, does she?"

"Yeah. And she says your hands shake and—"

"Noralee, you shouldn't believe everything your sister tells you. Just ask yourself, how would *she* know?"

"Oh, Edith says she knows everything."

"You believe that?"

Noralee studied the type stick cradled in her palm. "I dunno. That's why I asked you."

Cole studied the girl's earnest face, then let his gaze drift out the front window. *How* did *you know when you fall in love?* Talk about a punch straight into his gut. Oh, shoot, he didn't want to remember.

"Mr. Sanders?"

"Well, um…"

"And don't tell me you just *know*. That's what Ma always says, but I think she says that cuz *she* doesn't really know."

"Why wouldn't your mother know? She married your father, didn't she?"

"Yeah, but… But I think she did it just cuz Pa kept askin' her. Not cuz she was in love. And that's what Pa thinks, too."

"Noralee, usually when people get married they care about each other. It might not be all flutters and blushes, but it's real all the same."

"How do you know, Mr. Sanders? You ever loved anybody?"

Cole shut his eyes. God yes, he'd loved somebody. And his heart had pounded and his head had gone fuzzy and all the rest. It had been the most earth-shaking thing that had ever happened to him, and he knew right down to the bottom of his boots that he would never, ever forget it.

Or her. He swallowed over a sharp rock lodged in his throat and opened his eyes.

"Well," he said. He cleared his throat. "Well, I think that, um, you should be sure to take your pulse every morning to check your heartbeat and see if you can remember your multiplication tables to check your brain."

"Oh."

"You any good at math?"

"Well, yes, but..."

"Okay, figure me this—how many articles can you typeset in an hour?"

"Depends on how long the articles are."

"Right. Now, about—"

"You gonna answer my question, Mr. Sanders?" She poked out her lower lip and swung her heel against the stool rung.

"Look, Noralee, I'm not going to lie to you. When you fall in love you'll feel it in every single part of you, your head, your heart, right down to your big toe. You won't be able to miss it."

Her brown eyes widened. "Really? Really and truly?"

"Really and truly."

"Does it ever go away?"

"No, honey, it doesn't ever go away. So be careful who you fall in love with, you hear?"

He had to clear his throat again, but it didn't help. He could see Maryann in that blue gingham dress he loved, coming through the apple orchard as she always did when he worked late on the newspaper, and a sharp ache knifed into his belly.

He wondered if he'd ever be able to think of her without feeling as if he'd been hit over the head with a spiked shovel. Two spiked shovels.

Probably not. But Noralee didn't need to know that love hurt like hell and you never got over it. Noralee was only what, eleven years old? Plenty of time to get her young heart trampled to bits.

"You fancy a sarsaparilla?" he asked.

"Sure, Mr. Sanders."

"I'll bring one from the Golden Partridge."

He bolted for the door and the shot of whiskey waiting to ease that damn pain in his gut.

Chapter Eight

"What about it, Sanders?" Conway Arbuckle pounded his fist on Cole's desk, right on top of Jessamine's latest editorial. "You gonna let that stuck-up *Sentinel* woman get away with that tripe she wrote about me?"

Cole stood up and turned his head to one side to avoid the man's beery breath. "Nothing libelous about her words, Arbuckle. Just pointed." He exhaled. "And blunt."

"Blunt! She's like a poker banging into my hide. What are you gonna do about it?"

"Nothing, yet. The *Lark* doesn't come out until Friday."

"Nothing! Either you cut that she-witch down to size or I'll…"

Cole raised one eyebrow. "Don't threaten me, Arbuckle."

The man snapped his mouth shut, pivoted and

stomped out the door. Behind him, Noralee coughed politely.

"That man's still got really bad breath."

Cole laughed. "You don't like Arbuckle much, do you, Noralee?"

"No. And it isn't just his breath. He's mean. What are you going to do, Mr. Sanders?"

Cole thought that one over. True, Jessamine's latest editorial had hit hard on Arbuckle's weak spots, his blustery attitude, his arrogance, his preference for insulting his opponent personally rather than engaging the sheriff on specific issues.

He scanned the editorial again. "Bombastic...barbarian...bully..." Seemed she preferred the *B* words this week. Made for poetic reading matter, but she was skating on thin ice.

Well, so what? Let her punch a hole in the ice and sink. In this business she had to learn to be not only smart but tough. If the intrepid young editor of the *Sentinel* wanted to take potshots at Arbuckle, let her. And let her pay the piper.

Anyway, two could play at that game. He picked up his pen.

Jessamine slept late, bone-tired after scrambling to get the Wednesday edition of the *Sentinel* written, printed, folded and stuffed into Teddy's saddlebags and Billy Rowell's over-the-shoulder sack and then studying the soprano vocal part for tonight's rehearsal.

Her small upstairs bedroom was freezing cold, and while she could hear Eli chunking wood into the potbellied stove downstairs in her office, she knew the heat wouldn't penetrate to the second floor for at least an hour. She snuggled down under the double layer of quilts and waited for the sun to hit the windows and warm up the room.

Oh, botheration! She'd have to get out of bed to raise the window shades to catch the morning sunshine. Clutching a quilt about her shivering body, she crept out of bed and across the room, snapped up both shades and peered out.

Oh, my stars! Directly opposite her, framed in the window above the *Lark* office across the street, stood Cole Sanders. And mercy! He wore nothing but his— She tugged down the shade. Then she thoughtfully bit her lip. If she could see him, then he could see her! But she always closed her shades at night, so he couldn't possibly…

Oh, but he could. Each night she undressed by the light of her kerosene lamp, and that meant Cole was in a good position to see her naked body silhouetted against the window covering.

Why, that…that…no-account devil! Surely there was something in Sheriff Silver's law books about spying on a woman? Hurriedly she pulled on her drawers and camisole, tied her petticoat around her waist, and donned a dark green wool skirt and a clean shirtwaist.

Then she paused and swallowed hard. Before accusing him, she would have to check her facts. She would wait until he left his office for breakfast, then sneak across the street to the *Lark* office and check out the view from Mr. Sanders's upstairs window. *She was learning.*

At ten o'clock she watched Cole saunter off down the boardwalk toward the restaurant, and she grabbed her coat, sped across the street and made a beeline for the *Lark* office.

The room upstairs was a mirror image of hers except that the bed was on the opposite wall, and he used fruit crates for bookcases and his washbasin was tin, not china, like hers.

She advanced to his window. Just as she suspected; he could see directly into her bedroom across the way. She knew it! At night he would be able to see her shadow behind the drawn blinds and...

Downstairs the door clicked open, and every nerve and muscle in her body froze. Then the door closed and she heard the woodstove grate open, wood being chunked in, and Cole's voice humming. Clementine again.

She would wait it out. She tiptoed over to the narrow cot and very quietly sat down on the rumpled quilt.

An hour went by. Then two. More humming, and

a chuckle or two. He must be writing articles for his newspaper.

By noon she was so hungry her stomach began to growl loudly enough she was sure he would hear it. Could she open the window and climb out? Would a drop from the second floor kill her? Or just break her legs?

She twisted toward the window and accidentally knocked a book off one of the fruit crates beside the cot.

The humming downstairs stopped. Jessamine held her breath and clasped both arms over her belly to muffle the gurgling. *Please, Lord, rescue me from this embarrassing predicament.* Heavy footsteps sounded up the stairs, and in the next instant Cole Sanders loomed in his bedroom doorway.

"Jessamine! What the hell are you doing up here?"

Jess quailed at the outrage in his voice. What excuse could she possibly offer?

She could lie.

No, she couldn't.

She could cry.

No, she couldn't. Tears would be just as much a lie.

"I—I wanted to check what you could see from your window."

He propped his hands on his hips. "Yeah? What *can* you see from my window?"

"I can see straight into *my* bedroom window."

He nodded. "So, now you know."

"I should think you would deny it," she muttered.

"Not likely. You're intelligent. Observant. And curious. You'd have it figured out in a matter of seconds."

"Well, yes, I did figure it out."

"And you want me to apologize."

"I want you to stop spying on me."

He gave her a lopsided smile. "It's a free country, Jessamine. You don't own the view from my window."

"Well! You have a lot of nerve. I'll—I'll report you to Sheriff Silver."

"Go ahead. Know what he'll say?"

She shook her head.

He laughed. "He'll tell you to undress in the dark."

She couldn't look at him. Somehow her presence in his bedroom sent her pulse skittering. A heavy silence fell.

Cole took a single step into the room. "Jessamine, it's not illegal for a man to admire a woman's body." He waited, but she said nothing.

"Don't undress in the dark, Jess. You're beautiful. I'm not going to apologize for noticing that."

He moved another step into the room and reached one hand to touch her shoulder. "But you'd better get out of my bedroom. Might give Noralee the wrong idea."

All the way down the stairs and out the front door she heard his rich, gentle laughter. It made her spine tingle.

Rita Sheltonberg planted her feet heavily in front of Jess's desk and leaned over the high roll-top. "Miss Jessamine, we gotta do something more for Johnny."

"Johnny? Who is Johnny?"

"You know, Jericho. Sheriff Silver. When he decided to run for district judge, I volunteered to be his campaign manager, but I've plumb run out of things to do."

Jessamine smiled at the still-handsome older woman. "Seems to me you're doing a good job of spreading the word, Rita. I've seen the posters you put up all over town."

"Nice, aren't they? Kids at the schoolhouse made 'em for an art project. 'Cast Your Vote for the Battle of Jericho.' Kinda catchy, isn't it?"

"Yes, catchy," Jess agreed. "The trouble is, Mr. Arbuckle is putting up posters, too. 'A Vote for Arbuckle Is a Vote for Good Government, Like Good Coffee.'"

"I don't get it," the waitress blurted out.

"Mr. Arbuckle's grandfather is the founder of Arbuckle's Coffee."

"Oh, *that* Arbuckle. I'll have to make sure the hotel restaurant changes brands right away."

"There's money behind his campaign, Rita. And he's finagled the support of the *Lark* newspaper but— Wait a minute! I have an idea."

"Oh? What's that?"

"Yes, a wonderful idea. Rita, you just leave everything to me."

When Rita left to return to the restaurant, Jess grabbed her coat and scarf. Eli planted himself in her path.

"Hold on a minute, Jess. Last time you had a 'wonderful idea,' the ranchers and the sheep men in this county 'bout came to gunplay."

"This," she said, patting his arm where he'd shoved up the sleeves of his baggy sweater, "is an even more wonderful idea."

"Criminy," he muttered as the office door slammed. "Guess I'd better mosey on down to the mercantile and get some more cartridges for my forty-four."

Cole trotted Dancer alongside Teddy MacAllister's roan mare as they rode toward the Sorensen ranch. The minute they reached the edge of the spread, Cole reined up.

"Want to trade mounts, Teddy? I mean Ted?" The boy was trying so hard to grow up it made Cole's insides hurt.

"Sure do, Mr. Sanders." The boy slipped off his roan and clambered up onto Cole's Arabian. They rode in companionable silence for a mile before Teddy spoke.

"Kin I ask you something, Mr. Sanders?"

"What about?"

"Girls."

Cole disguised his surprise with a cough. First Noralee and now Teddy. Guess he was the "go-to" source for youngsters wondering what life was all about. "Fire away, son."

Teddy thought for a long minute. "Well, uh, how do you know when a girl likes you?"

Cole coughed again. "Most times you don't. You have some particular girl in mind?"

"Um, yeah. Her name's Manette Nicolet. She's French. Talks foreign words all the time."

"And what do you do?"

"Aw, I can't talk French. Sometimes I bring her bugs 'n' stuff."

"Bugs?"

"Yeah. She likes crawly things. Insects, you know?"

Cole rolled his eyes. "Interesting female."

"Yeah, and she's real pretty, too."

"Figures," Cole said under his breath.

"So, how do I know if she likes me?"

Cole pulled the roan into an even slower walk and sucked in a gulp of air. "You don't, Ted. You might never know how she feels about you. But if you're smart, you'll treat her real special, no matter what."

Teddy thought for a few minutes. "Is that what you do?"

"Well, yeah. If I get the chance, that is."

"Miss Jessamine's kinda temperamental, huh?"

Cole barked out a laugh. "Kinda." God, was it that obvious he was attracted to the *Sentinel*'s prim and proper editor?

"My advice," Teddy said with a conspiratorial wink, "is to bring her some bugs."

When Cole rode back into town with the boy, he couldn't help glancing at the front window of the *Sentinel* office. Bugs, huh? He'd have to give Teddy's suggestion some thought.

He reined his sleek Arabian to a stop and approached the hitching rail just as Jessamine stepped out of her office and hailed him.

"Cole, I need to talk to you."

"What's up?" he asked carefully.

"I have an idea."

Cole rolled his eyes. "Not another one. Eli told me about the Sheepmen's Summit meeting last spring."

"Eli talks entirely too much. Get down off your horse and listen for a minute."

He swung down and stood with the reins in one hand. "Okay, I'm listening."

Jess tried not to watch his supple fingers holding the leather lines. "Your candidate and my candidate are just trading insults in your newspaper and mine. What if they met face-to-face and argued in person?"

"A debate, you mean?"

"Exactly. What do you think?"

"Good idea," he said with a nod. "When? The election's getting close."

"Next Monday night? At the church meeting hall. We could—"

"Arrange for a moderator," he finished for her. "Someone—"

"Like Matt Johnson, Ellie's husband," Jess interrupted. "He's a federal marshal, and—"

"He'd be armed," Cole inserted. "Nobody would dare speak out of turn."

"I'll talk it up in the *Sentinel* and—"

"I'll do the same in the *Lark*," he finished. He removed his black Stetson and held it over his heart. "Great minds—"

"Are never at a loss. Oh, Cole, it will be fun!"

"And a challenge," he added. "Once Arbuckle gets going, he's hard to shut up."

"Jericho Silver can shut him up," she said smugly. "Just you wait and see."

Just before the next chorus rehearsal, winter struck with a vengeance. All afternoon rain spit against the front window of the *Lark* office, and by suppertime the sky had turned black and hail was bouncing off the boardwalk.

At the restaurant, Cole downed a bowl of hot chili and a slab of apple pie, then snugged up his jacket and started off for the music school rehearsal room. Halfway down the boardwalk, he spied Jessamine trudging along ahead of him.

"Can't hardly sing if our teeth are chattering," he remarked from three paces behind her.

"'Can't hardly'? Heavens, such grammar!" She turned toward him and teetered on the hail-spattered planks. Just as she lost her balance, he snaked out an arm, caught her shoulder and held on while she righted herself.

"I hate winter," she gasped.

"I've always liked it." He slid his arm around her waist and urged her forward. "Rain makes the corn grow and flowers bloom in the spring. Anything ungrammatical in that?"

She laughed, and he expelled a sigh of relief. Maybe she wasn't so prickly on rehearsal nights. Or maybe she was just too cold to talk back. Whatever it was, he liked it when she was quiet.

Actually, he liked it when she talked back, too.

After their vocal warm-ups, the director stopped them and made a surprising announcement. "Ladies, on choir rehearsal nights, please dispense with your corsets. You cannot breathe properly when you are all trussed up in whalebone."

Cole had a hard time keeping his mind off Jessamine's body with no corset.

The director rehearsed them rigorously for an hour, let them take a break, then pushed them even harder. Halfway through the last chorus, something intangible swept through the singers, as if a single bolt of lightning had struck them all simultaneously. The sounds they made were suddenly tinged with magic, and in the middle of the chorale they were singing, they looked at each other in wonder.

Ellie Johnson's usually impassive expression melted into dazed surprise, and on impulse Cole turned slightly so he could see Jessamine's face.

Her mouth was rounded into a soft, rosy O, and her green eyes were wide-open and bright with un-shed tears. A fist slammed into his chest.

His throat closed up so tight he couldn't sing if his life depended on it, but it didn't matter. The swell of the music swept them all up into one of those rare moments when everything came together in perfection.

Mercy, it was almost like an orgasm.

His gaze met Jessamine's, and he stopped breathing. Suddenly he wanted to hold her. Touch her. *He wanted to make love to her.*

His own eyes stung. Whoa, what was happening?

When the chorale ended, the director stood transfixed, and no one spoke for a long minute.

"That," Ellie said at last, "does not happen very often. We are attaining something magnificent in this music. Something important."

She dismissed the choir members early. People were unusually quiet as they pulled on coats and gloves and bid each other good-night. Cole was still shaken by what had hit him. He caught Jessamine at the door and waylaid her with a hand on her shoulder.

"Walk you home?" he said quietly. She nodded and wound her blue knit scarf over her ears and around her chin.

When they stepped outside, she gave a little cry. "Look! It's snowing!"

Sure enough, powdery flakes were sifting down, dusting the street, the trees, even her hair with white lace. Sounds were muffled. It was magical, an enchantment of gauzy flakes.

Even their footsteps were softened by the silence. He'd seen snow before. He'd ridden in it, walked in it, but it had never looked this beautiful before. It made him feel humble, even reverent, right down to his boot tops.

They didn't speak, and when her foot slipped on the slick boardwalk, he caught her around the waist and they moved on in step together. When they reached the *Sentinel* office, Cole withdrew his arm.

Jessamine gestured toward the snow-dusted pines beyond the main street. "It's beautiful, isn't it?" she murmured.

"It is." But he wasn't looking at the trees. He was looking straight into her eyes. "Beautiful."

"Good night, Cole."

"'Night, Jessamine."

Jess studied his oddly strained visage a long moment, then turned toward the front door of her office. She should remind him about the candidates' debate on Monday, but she couldn't make herself speak such mundane words. It would only remind him, remind them both, that they were on opposite sides.

He couldn't know how desperate she felt about the survival of the *Sentinel*, how much she resented his coming here to Smoke River and threatening her livelihood. The *Sentinel* was her whole reason for being.

She was so afraid of failing, of finding out she didn't have the intelligence or the skill or the grit to be a true journalist. Most of the time she felt like a failure, especially since Cole Sanders had arrived in Smoke River. He obviously knew what he was doing as a newspaperman. She did not.

She had worked hard to learn things from Miles, and she had to work even harder now that she was on her own. Failure shadowed every word she put down on her yellow notepad, every article she wrote. With each issue of her newspaper she shuddered with apprehension lest someone march into her office and fire a gun into her chest, as someone had done to Miles.

Tonight she wanted to forget, just for a moment. Forget her fears and the barrier that lay between Cole Sanders and herself.

Suddenly she heard his voice behind her. "Jess?"

She swung back toward him and a soft, slushy snowball landed on her cheek.

"Leave your lamp on tonight."

She wanted to laugh. She wanted to heave a snowball right back at him, to forget everything but the lovely, silent night and the delicious fleeting camaraderie between them. It made her hungry for something she couldn't put into words.

All at once she found that her eyes were stinging.

Chapter Nine

The debate between Sheriff Jericho Silver and his opponent, Conway Arbuckle, drew townspeople, ranchers, sheepmen and farmers from as far north as Gillette Springs. They thronged the church meeting hall, arguing at the tops of their lungs. Even the women's voices were raised.

The hall echoed with accusations and recriminations until Federal Marshal Matt Johnson, seated at a long table, gaveled the crowd into quiet.

Jessamine sat on one end of the oak table, Cole on the other, watching as the marshal rose to open the proceedings. Opponents Silver and Arbuckle sat across the room at opposite ends of another table.

"Listen up," Matt called. "We're all here for a peaceable debate between the two candidates for district judge. Both the editor of the *Smoke River Sentinel*, Miss Jessamine Lassiter, and the *Lake County Lark* editor, Mr. Cole Sanders, have submitted questions for Mr. Silver and Mr. Arbuckle. I will read the question aloud, and then each candidate will have two minutes to respond."

The marshal ostentatiously produced an egg timer filled with sand and set it on the table before him. Jess choked back a laugh. Next, he unfolded a scrap of paper with the first question scrawled on it.

"Mr. Arbuckle, would you tell those assembled here what you feel your qualifications are for the office of district judge?"

Conway Arbuckle, in a natty gray pin-striped suit and an emerald bow tie, stood up, stuck his thumbs in his vest pockets and cleared his throat.

"First, I am a legitimate, I repeat, *legitimate* attorney-at-law. Second, I am a college graduate. My education was obtained at, ahem, Hahvard College."

Jess eyed Cole and they both began scribbling furiously on their notepads. What was he writing? She'd give a cookie to peek over his shoulder, but she wasn't close enough. Instead she studied his right hand, now flicking his pencil back and forth between his thumb and forefinger.

Oh, good, he was nervous. She hoped he was afraid of what she might write about Arbuckle in the Wednesday edition of the *Sentinel*. She liked making Cole nervous. She especially liked it when she licked her lips and his breath hitched in. It made her feel powerful, but at the same time shaky inside, not calm and ice-minded as a newspaper editor should be. It made her feel vulnerable somehow, as if…as if what Cole thought of her mattered.

But of course what Cole Sanders thought about her mattered no more than a puff of dandelion fuzz.

Of course.

"Thirdly," Arbuckle droned on, his voice rising into speech-making mode, "I support law and order. As judge I intend to prosecute lawbreakers to the full extent of my God-given authority."

He settled back into his chair with a self-satisfied smirk.

The marshal gaveled the buzzing crowd into silence, then turned to Jericho. "Sheriff Silver?"

Jericho Silver shoved to his feet. His jeans were clean, his leather vest well-worn and his boots still bore spurs that chinked when he moved. He respectfully removed his well-worn black Stetson and faced the crowd.

"I have to admit I am not an attorney. I have taken the qualifying exam, but I won't know the results until Christmas. I also have to say that I've never been to college. But I have studied the set of law books my wife, Maddie, gave me when we were married."

Cole sent her an enigmatic smile and flipped to a new page in his notebook.

"As for dealing with lawbreakers," the sheriff continued, "I figure every man, or woman, is assumed innocent until proved guilty. And in my view, punishment should be fair and swift."

Murmurs went around the room. Good for him, Jess thought. She admired Sheriff Silver. When Miles was killed, Jericho Silver had tracked the murderer for four days and brought him back for trial. He also kept a sharp eye out for her during those first few months after she'd taken over the newspaper. Even now she knew she could count on Jericho Silver to deter harassment from an out-of-sorts subscriber.

Cole Sanders was backing the wrong candidate, plain and simple.

"Next question," Matt said. "What is your family background, Mr. Arbuckle?"

Arbuckle leaped to his feet. "My great-grandparents were among the first settlers in this great country. They established substantial tobacco plantations in Virginia. My mother was a Phelan, Irish Catholic, ya know. My daddy, well, let's just say the Arbuckle name, and the brew you all drink every morning speaks for itself."

Jess heard Cole mutter something under his breath. It sounded like "Big shot."

When Arbuckle sat down, Jericho stood up and looked directly at the audience members.

"I don't know who my parents were," he said evenly. "Either my mother or father may have been Indian, but I don't know that for sure. I guess you'd have to call me an orphan. I came to Smoke River when I ran away from the orphanage in Portland.

Must have been about ten or maybe eleven years old. I've never really known when my birthday was."

"Huh!" Arbuckle scoffed. "The man's nuthin' but a half-breed!"

"Very likely," Jericho said in a quiet voice. "That doesn't make me any less an American than anybody else."

At that, the onlookers cheered, and Marshal Johnson gaveled for silence. Jessamine peeked over at Cole, who sat stroking his chin. He wasn't smiling.

"Next question," the marshal announced. "What does the word *justice* mean to you? Arbuckle?"

Instantly Arbuckle was on his feet, his arms waving. "Justice is the great American tradition of making sure the punishment fits the…er…crime. And making sure red-blooded Americans get their fair share of everything they're entitled to."

Jessamine shot another look at Cole and began a new page of notes.

"Mr. Silver?"

The sheriff took a minute to collect his thoughts and then rose. "Justice is what every man, rich or poor, white or Indian or Negro or Chinese or Mexican or anything else, is entitled to under the American Constitution."

More cheers. Cole pinned Jessamine with narrowed eyes so dark a blue they looked like muddy ink. Her stomach gave an unexpected lurch. Something in her opponent's gaze sent her pulse skittering. Why, he looked mad enough to— "Well, shoot, folks," Arbuckle yelled. "That definition's pretty broad, isn't it? That means *anybody* could—"

The marshal's gavel cut him off. With a lifted eyebrow in Jess's direction, Cole ripped a page out of his notepad and stuffed it into his shirt pocket.

"Next question," the marshal announced. "How would you describe your constituency, the people of Lake County? Mr. Arbuckle?"

"Glad to, glad to." Arbuckle rose and puffed out his chest. "I'd say my constituency consists of the good people of Lake County, and that includes the fair communities of Gillette Springs and Smoke River folks. We're all upright, God-fearing, clean-living folks. Which makes our fair neck of the great state of Oregon one of the best, most industrious, most hardworking, most law-abiding places it's my privilege to serve."

"Ye're not servin' it yet," someone yelled. Jessamine lowered her head to hide a smile. When she looked up, Cole was staring at her. It made her so nervous she couldn't think.

The marshal gaveled for quiet. "Mr. Silver?"

Jess sat with her pencil poised as the sheriff slowly stood up and turned sideways to include those seated in back of him. "I think people in Lake County are like people everywhere, no better, no worse. I would hope to serve them all equally and fairly."

Arbuckle grew red in the face. "Selling these good folks kinda short, aren't you, Sheriff?"

"Shaddup, Arbuckle!" This echoed from the far corner of the packed room. Jessamine peered in that direction, but she couldn't identify the shouter. She exchanged another look with Cole, who shrugged and pocketed a second sheet of notepaper.

My! He seemed to be taking lots and lots of notes. She scanned the few pages she'd filled in her own notepad, praying her memory could fill in any gaps. She couldn't ever remember feeling so flat-footed when it came to note-taking. Was her mind wandering? Worse, was she exposing herself as a fraud in the business of journalism?

"Last question," the marshal announced. "Let's say that while we're all sitting here tonight the Smoke River Bank is robbed. What would you do? Arbuckle—?"

The man was on his feet before Matt finished speaking.

"First I'd alert the marshal. That'd be you, Marshal Johnson. Then I'd make sure they got up a good posse, and then I'd be the first one to join it."

"Bull hockey," a man shouted.

Arbuckle turned red. "Whaddya mean by that, mister? That's exactly what I'd do, and don't you forget it!"

"Sheriff Silver?" the marshal queried in a calm voice.

Again, Jericho took his time answering. "If the bank was robbed tonight while we're all sitting here and I was serving as district judge, I'd keep right on sitting here. A district judge has no authority to contact a federal marshal or the sheriff or anybody else. And that goes for forming a posse, or joining one, for that matter. A judge has a duty to weigh evidence in a trial. He should consider the facts, not take sides."

The audience went wild, whistling and pounding their feet on the floor. Cole tore up his notes and scattered the pieces, then bent forward, peered around Marshal Johnson and mouthed something to Jessamine.

"Let's get out of here."

Without a word she stuffed her notepad into her skirt pocket, pushed back her chair and headed for the door.

Conway Arbuckle lumbered into Cole's path. "Well, Sanders? Whaddya think?"

Cole pushed past him. "Not much." He caught up with Jessamine on the church steps outside.

"Jessamine. Slow down."

She whirled to face him, her green eyes heated. "I'm too mad to slow down. How can you stomach that man's drivel?"

"Whiskey helps," he quipped.

"Unfortunately I cannot frequent the Golden Partridge, but oh! If I weren't a lady, I would—"

"Doesn't Eli keep a bottle of something around the office?"

"Well, yes, but—"

"Come on." He grabbed her hand and pulled her down the boardwalk to the *Sentinel* office. For the past half hour he'd tried to keep his eyes off Jessamine, tried not to notice when she caught her lower lip between her teeth and worried it into a raspberry flush.

He needed a drink.

Inside her office she unwound her scarf while Cole lit the kerosene lamp and unearthed Eli's whiskey flask, which the old man kept in a cabinet under his typesetting table. Cole popped out the cork, wiped the bottle neck on his shirt and handed it to her.

"I don't usually indulge in spirits," she said with a laugh.

"Indulge," he ordered. "Takes the bad taste out of your mouth." And maybe it'd help him sleep tonight. It wasn't the debate that had his chest tight; it was the editor of his rival newspaper. Damn, all she had to do was smile at him to twist his belly into a knot.

She tipped the bottle, swallowed once and coughed until tears came into her eyes. Cole grasped it and gulped down a double mouthful.

"I hate that man!" she fumed. She upended the flask and swallowed another mouthful, choked, then handed it back to him.

He looked at her, took another hit and slowly lowered the bottle. "You hate Arbuckle worse than you hate me?"

"Of course worse than you. Cole, I don't hate you, I—"

"You sure?" He downed another gulp.

She looked at him oddly. "Of course I'm sure."

"In that case…" Carefully he set the flask on her desk and bent to blow out the lantern.

"Cole? What are you doing?"

"You've been biting your lips all evening, and I can't stand it one more minute." He tipped her chin up with his forefinger. "Close your eyes, Jess."

He caught her mouth under his.

Mercy alive, what am I doing? Women had been permanently off his list since Maryann died, so why couldn't he stop? Kissing Jessamine made him so hungry and light-headed he wondered if he was dreaming. Or crazy. *Yeah, definitely crazy.*

"Jess," he whispered when he could breathe again.

"We're enemies," she said in a dazed voice. "Aren't we?"

"Not hardly," he said, his voice hoarse. "We just run two opposing newspapers, and we probably have different opinions on just about everything, but for damn sure we're not enemies."

He kissed her again. "Opponents, maybe," he murmured, "but not enemies."

After a long, long time she stirred in his arms. "Is there any more whiskey?" she said in a shaky voice.

"Probably. You don't need it."

"Oh, but I—"

"Trust me, Jess. We've both had enough." He held her against him, his breathing ragged, then deliberately set her apart and strode out the door.

Jess stood without moving, touching her lips with her fingers and wondering what had just happened.

That night she dreamed she was walking through an ice-encrusted forest, feeling inexplicably light and happy, and warmed by a presence she could not see.

Cole bent over Jessamine's latest *Sentinel* editorial page spread out on his desk and groaned under his breath. "… A self-righteous puffed-up politician with bread crumbs for brains and a peculiarly selfish predilection for boring his listeners."

Whew! Not libel, but close. And today she seemed to be stuck on *P* words. *Puffed up. Pretentious. Predilection.* He'd have to print some sort of rebuttal before Arbuckle went on the warpath.

He stroked his chin and began to plan the first page of his next edition. But after the other night's encounter with Jess, he discovered he couldn't put two thoughts together in a logical sequence.

Jessamine looked up to see Rosie Greywolf glide past the front window of the *Sentinel* office, glance to her right, then left, and slip noiselessly through the front door. The Indian woman washed dishes at the restaurant and was raising her two boys in a tiny cabin just outside town.

"Psssst, missy!"

"Good morning, Rosie. What can I do for you?"

"Is what I can do for you, missy. You listen."

"Yes?" Intrigued, Jessamine leaned forward. "I'm listening."

Rosie studied Eli, seated on his stool, with suspicious black eyes. "That one safe?"

"Eli? Oh, yes, he is 'safe.' Eli works for my newspaper."

"No repeat?"

"Repeat what, Rosie? Tell me what you came to say."

The woman twitched her long calico skirt. "I know something about Mr. Coffee Man."

"You mean Mr. Arbuckle?"

"He big sneak. Have two wives."

A snort erupted from Eli at the font case.

"Hush, Eli. Rosie, what makes you think Mr. Arbuckle has two wives?"

"I also work at hotel. Coffee man live at hotel."

"And?"

"Live at hotel with one wife. Sleep in big house in town with other wife."

"Ha!" Eli burst out. "Got hisself a wh—a fancy lady."

Rosie nodded. "Hotel wife flat here." She pointed

to her ample bosom. "Other wife…" She made a curving gesture with both hands. "More like Rosie."

Eli practically crowed. "Pretty juicy item, huh, Jess?"

"Eli, do be quiet."

"You tell this in newspaper?" Rosie whispered.

"Rosie, I can't print this. It's hearsay."

"No, missy. Is *see*-say. I see. You say."

Jess sighed. She would dearly love to libel Mr. Arbuckle, but that was just what it would be, libel. As a responsible journalist she couldn't print a word of it. "Rosie, I am sorry. But thank you for keeping your eyes open."

The Indian woman leaned closer. "Hear much at hotel. I keep watch for you." With that, she slipped quietly out the door and moved past the front window and on down the boardwalk.

"Too bad ya cain't spread that all over page one, Jess. That'd fix Arbuckle's wagon good."

"I've already fixed his wagon, Eli. You typeset my editorial about Mr. Arbuckle yesterday. I couldn't have been more pointed about that bloated—"

She broke off as Conway Arbuckle's bulky form barreled into her office. He stomped up to her desk and shook his pudgy fist in her face.

"You're gonna regret the day you wrote that tripe about me," he yelled. He slapped yesterday's *Sentinel* editorial on her desk.

Slowly Jess forced herself to stand erect. If he was going to shoot her, he'd have a gun, wouldn't he?

"No, Mr. Arbuckle, I do not regret what I wrote. The public has every right to—"

"Don't you talk back to me, you little bitch!"

Before she could draw breath, Arbuckle pulled a shiny revolver out of his jacket pocket and aimed it straight at her heart.

"Eli," she said, keeping her gaze fixed on the weapon, "get down behind the press."

Arbuckle's gun wavered. "Either you print a retraction or—"

"Or you will shoot me?" She didn't like the crazed look in his watery eyes, but she worked to keep her voice steady.

"Damn straight. Start writing!"

"I am afraid I c-cannot do that."

He waved the weapon in her face, then dropped the barrel to point once more at her chest. "You can, and by God you will."

Jess remembered the look on Miles's face when he had been shot, as if he was surprised. Lord have mercy, she would look just like that. All at once she couldn't breathe, couldn't think. She wasn't surprised; she was terrified. She wanted to be a good journalist, but oh, God, she didn't want to die. She closed her eyes and tried to focus.

And then she heard Cole's voice. "Drop it, Arbuckle."

He stood framed in the doorway, a rifle aimed at Arbuckle's spine. The man swung toward the door, but Cole stepped forward and knocked Arbuckle's gun arm upward. The revolver arced out of his grasp and clattered onto the floor. Cole kicked it away, then smashed the rifle butt into the man's jaw.

Jessamine yelped. Cole looked over to see her holding Eli's brass spittoon aloft. "Oh," she said. And then "Oh," again.

He yanked Arbuckle to his feet and pulled his red face up close to his. "If I ever see you in this office again, I'll kill you. You got that?"

"S-sure, Sanders. Just a little misunderstanding between the lady and—"

Before he could finish, Cole booted him out onto the boardwalk.

"You okay, Eli?" he called.

"Yo," came a quavery voice.

Cole scooped up Arbuckle's gun and stepped behind the press. "Eli, can you handle a revolver?"

"Yep. Fought Indians one summer after the war, till I...well, I deserted. I keep a forty-four back of my font case, but I couldn't get to it in time."

"Keep this one in your belt." He laid the weapon in Eli's unsteady hand. Then he moved to a frozen Jess and lifted the spittoon out of her hands. "What were you going to do with this anyway?"

"H-hit him over the head. I was afraid he was going to sh-shoot you."

He just looked at her.

"Thank you, Cole. Thank you."

He nodded. "It was a good editorial, Jess."

"Th-thank you," she said again.

"Choir rehearsal again tonight," he reminded her. "And don't forget," he said with a smile, "no corset."

Eli haw-hawed from his stool behind the press, and Jessamine started to bite her lips.

Cole sighed. "And for God's sake," he murmured, "don't do that, Jess. Otherwise I'm going to have another damn long night."

Chapter Ten

Cole sat at his desk, staring down at nothing and tried to order his brain to behave. It got like this sometimes, especially when he was stirred up about something. He was more than a little surprised that it was Jessamine Lassiter that triggered his memory this time.

It had been a long, hot day, the kind of day Quantrill had favored for his raids. Only Quantrill came at night, when there was no moon and mothers and fathers had tucked their little ones in bed.

The man liked fire, liked setting them. Some said he liked watching them burn. And he liked the sound of women screaming.

Don't think about it. Don't remember.

He tried to even out his breathing, but he couldn't control the panic. The feeling of helplessness. And the impotent, searing rage that poured over him when he remembered how it had been.

Maryann. Maryann, I tried. I tried so hard.

On days like this he wished it had been him. He'd begged God to let it have been him.

But He had taken Maryann instead.

The next night, Cole stopped in at the Golden Partridge, ordered a shot of whiskey and nursed it while keeping his ears open to the talk going on around him. Often while lounging at the bar he uncovered a lead on a good story.

"Not much support for Conway Arbuckle after his debate with Sheriff Silver," the stocky barkeep intoned while topping up his shot glass.

"What else do you hear?"

O'Reilly leaned over the polished wood bar. "Couple of sleazy-lookin' types behind you, talkin' kinda dirty about the *Sentinel*."

"You know them?"

"Nope. Never seen 'em before."

Cole studied the reflections of the two men in the mirror behind the bar. Unshaven. Sweat-soaked hats with brims curled up like dried orange peels. Filthy-looking leather vests. And, he noted with a jolt of alarm, both were packing revolvers.

As he watched, a third man pushed through the batwing doors and sauntered across the room to join the other two. One stuck out a dusty boot and shoved a chair toward the newcomer.

Something about the trio made the back of Cole's

neck prickle. He tried to overhear their subdued conversation, but no luck. Their damn hats were tipped so low he couldn't even read their lips.

He motioned the bartender over. "How long have they been here, Tom?"

"Most of the night. Seemed like they were waitin' for that third one. I checked the horses tied out front earlier and they looked mighty played out."

"Anything else?"

"Well, yeah. One of 'em keeps askin' for my dirty bar rags. Funny thing, though, none of them's cleaning their weapons or anything else."

Cole swiveled to face the room, planted both elbows on the bar and hooked his boot heel over the brass rail. The third man had a bulge in his jacket pocket that Cole guessed was a concealed revolver.

His skin felt as if ants were crawling over his body. As he watched, the three men hunched close together over the table, talking low.

Cole turned back to Tom. "Think I'll pay a visit to Sheriff Silver."

"Good idea. Don't want any trouble here, even if it *is* Saturday night."

At the sheriff's office, Jericho Silver listened carefully but said little until Cole finished describing the three strangers who'd apparently just drifted into town.

"Sorry to disappoint you, Cole, but I can't lock up somebody just because he looks suspicious. And it's not illegal to carry a weapon. It's only illegal if he uses it."

"I see." The sheriff's explanation didn't satisfy Cole, but there wasn't a thing he could do about it.

The lawman stood up and donned his black Stetson. "I'll walk the streets twice more tonight, just to check things out."

"Thanks, Sheriff."

Even after a juicy steak and some apple pie at the restaurant, Cole couldn't stop thinking about those three disreputable-looking men. Couldn't shake the bad feeling down deep in his gut, either.

Back at the *Lark* office he finished writing his editorial for the Tuesday edition, then paced back and forth across the plank floor trying to shake the feeling of foreboding that hung over him. Finally he stuffed his pencils in the desk drawer and went up the stairs to his bedroom.

Not one chance in a thousand Jessamine would keep her lamp on while she undressed tonight, he reasoned. Made him wish she'd never found out.

He shucked his boots and stretched out on the cot without undressing, then lay staring out his uncurtained window to watch the moonlight sift through the clouds.

He must have dozed off, and then suddenly he was wide-awake. He lay still, listening. He could hear the wind singing through the trees, and a lone night owl *tuwhooed* from someone's rooftop.

Increasingly uneasy, he moved across to the window and quietly raised the sash. Must have been past midnight; the moon was just setting. From the saloon down the street came the faint sound of male laughter and someone plucking a banjo.

He leaned farther out the window, scanned the main street from one end to the other, then studied the *Sentinel* building across the way. Smoke curled out the metal stovepipe venting the potbellied stove in Jessamine's office. But something…

He narrowed his eyes. God, it wasn't just smoke. Flames were flickering behind the *Sentinel*'s front windows!

Fire. The *Sentinel* building was burning!

He jammed on his boots and clattered down the stairs.

Before he was out the front door and onto the boardwalk he started yelling. "Jess! Jess!"

He burst through the unlocked front door and was instantly enveloped in smoke. He couldn't breathe, couldn't see, but he could hear the hungry growl of the flames. He stumbled against Jessamine's rolltop desk, then clawed his way past the printing press. Flames licked at his knees, but he found the staircase and groped his way upward through the billowing smoke one agonizingly slow step at a time.

At the top of the stairs, he ran smack into her bedroom door. He kicked it open and plunged through the smoke until he stumbled blindly against the bed.

"Jess, wake up!"

He groped for her arm and yanked hard. "Get up! Quick!"

She moaned and gave a throaty cough. He shoved one hand under her shoulders and pulled her upright. "Stand up, Jess. Now!"

She managed to get her feet onto the floor and tried to rise, but she stumbled against him. He scooped her up, felt his way to the windows and jammed one elbow through the glass. Gulping in a lungful of fresh air, he knocked out the remaining pieces of jagged glass, then dipped his knees to force her head through.

"Take a big breath," he ordered. He heard her drag in a wheezy lungful. "Another!"

She obeyed. "Now hold your breath," he shouted. He tightened his hold on her and lurched down the stairs. Her office was engulfed in flames.

"Shut your eyes," he yelled. He drew in a huge gulp of smoke-laden air and held it, then dashed into the smoke. Man, it felt like the fires of hell.

He burst out the front door and gulped in cold, clean air.

Jessamine clung to him. "My press!" she cried. "My printing press, all Eli's font cases, even…" She coughed and sobbed all at once. "Even his spittoon," she wept.

The sound tore into his gut. "It's all right, Jess.

You're all right. You're safe. I'm taking you over to the *Lark* office."

A group of locals had gathered and were starting to tackle the flames. Cole stopped a bystander passing buckets of water to the blaze and asked him to let the sheriff know what had happened. But he said nothing else until he climbed the stairs up to his bedroom and pushed open the door. "I've got nowhere else to take you, Jess, so I hope you understand."

"Yes," she said, her voice breaking. He set her down in front of the window overlooking the street, and together they watched tongues of flame lick away at the inside of the *Sentinel* building.

"My newspaper," she sobbed. "Everything I've worked for is gone. What will I do now?"

Cole stood at her back, holding her shuddering body against his chest. "Rebuild," he said after a long minute. "In the meantime, you can use my press to print your newspaper."

Something exploded inside the flaming building across the street, and in that instant Cole knew what had caused the fire.

"What was that noise?" Jessamine choked out.

Cole groaned. "That was a crude incendiary device. In Kansas we called them Quantrill Cookies. They're made out of whiskey bottles and rags."

She looked at him sharply. "How do you know that?"

"I know. Quantrill burned down my house in Kansas City. My wife died in the fire."

"Oh, my God." Her knees buckled. "That's horrible!"

"Yeah," he said shortly. "It was."

She peered again out his window. "I can't believe this is happening. I just can't believe it." Tears sheened her cheeks.

"Those bastards," he muttered under his breath. "Probably working for Arbuckle. Should have shot them when I had the chance."

An ache lodged deep in his chest. He walked her over to his cot, sat her down and lifted her legs onto the quilt. She wore nothing but a long white nightgown, and he wrapped the blanket about her shoulders and eased her back until she lay quietly on his bed. Then he stretched out full length beside her.

"I want you to stay here tonight."

She nodded without speaking.

"Don't think about it anymore, Jess. Try to get some sleep." He wrapped his arms around her and tugged a second quilt over them. "In the morning we'll look at the damage."

This was a damn sorry way to take a woman to bed, he thought irrationally. A familiar pain bloomed under his breastbone and he tried not to think about Maryann.

In the morning, Cole left Jess sound asleep, curled up on her side with one hand folded under her chin, and slipped downstairs to the sheriff's office. He sure hoped Jericho Silver would catch up with whoever did this. Arbuckle was probably behind it. The sheriff agreed but said he needed proof.

Back in front of the still-smoking *Sentinel* office, Cole found Eli pacing up and down on the boardwalk, disbelief on his lined face.

"What the hell happened?" the old man asked.

"Place was firebombed," Cole answered.

"Huh? Why'd anybody wanna do that?"

"Revenge, maybe."

Eli snapped his bearded jaw shut.

When the old man dragged himself off to the restaurant for some coffee, Cole scrabbled through the burned-out debris and found Eli's font case, melted into a blob of twisted metal. To his surprise Jessamine's once shiny Adams press was soot-stained but intact.

The staircase was partially burned away, but he picked his way carefully up the steps to her bedroom. Maybe he could find some of her books or a dress or two. Smoke blackened the painted walls, and everything smelled so bad he gave up the idea. The books were scorched, and the clothes…she'd never wear them again.

At the mercantile he talked Carl Ness out of half a dozen apple crates, loaded up the contents of Jess's scorched file cabinet and lugged them across the street to his office. Then he arranged for Eli to work at the *Lark* office, where he could set type for Jessamine's *Sentinel* stories alongside Noralee.

That afternoon the ashen-faced editor of his rival newspaper went to stay at Ilsa Rowell's boardinghouse, and the next morning Jessamine arranged with Ike Bruhn at the sawmill for a carpenter and enough wood to make repairs. With steely resolve she forbade herself to think about the fire, or the possible reason for it, and focused instead on salvaging what she could of her shattered life.

On Friday morning Cole's *Lark* newspaper came out, and on Saturday, Jessamine's *Sentinel* was typeset, printed on Cole's Ramage press and distributed as usual by Billy Rowell and Teddy MacAllister.

Jess tried hard not to think any further than one day ahead. She tried even harder to forget about the night she'd spent on Cole's bed, wrapped in his arms while she wept. He'd offered to sleep on the floor, but she had clung to him. She'd needed his strength that night, and even now, despite the impropriety of the situation, she wasn't sorry.

That night she'd sensed his own fear as well as hers. She wondered if Cole had been shaken at the thought of losing her in the same way he had lost his wife back in Kansas.

On Sunday, Sheriff Silver rode back into town, and the jail had three new inmates. That same afternoon Cole went looking for Conway Arbuckle.

He found the man cowering in his hotel room behind his wife's chifforobe. Without a second thought, Cole laid him flat with one punch.

Chapter Eleven

For the next week Jessamine worked at the *Lark* office, close enough to Cole to read over his shoulder as he wrote his editorials. Trying to compose her own news stories felt like working in a fishbowl where her every sharpened pencil, every scratched-out word, every move she made was visible to him. The arrangement, she decided after the very first day, could never work. They were like two bumblebees trapped together in a jam jar.

It made her nervous being so near him. Hour after hour she found her attention straying across to his side of the room, which was more than a little embarrassing. Eli was watching. Noralee, too. She didn't want either of them, and especially not Cole, to know she was interested enough in what he was doing to surreptitiously watch him.

Then why are you?

She had no answer to that. At least not an answer

that made rational sense. She liked looking at him while he worked writing an article. A little frown would appear between his dark eyebrows, and when he was thinking about something, or when he was stuck, he rolled his pencil back and forth between his fingers.

Cole Sanders was extremely handsome, she admitted, with his unruly dark hair, firm jaw and piercing blue eyes. She wished she could concentrate on her work the way he did, but she liked looking at him too much.

She spent one whole day across the street in her burned-out office, scrubbing the smoke residue off her rolltop desk. The next afternoon she talked Whitey Poletti and Noralee's father, the mercantile owner, into muscling it across the street into the *Lark* office.

The next morning she washed every single smoke-smudged windowpane in her ruined office and swept out the mounds of sawdust left by the carpenter as he worked repairing the stairs leading up to her bedroom. When he was finished nailing the last plank, she ventured upstairs to inspect the damage.

The room still reeked of smoke. For a moment she felt physically sick knowing that someone had tried to burn down her newspaper. She would have died if Cole hadn't come for her.

She knew she would never forget that night. She still thought about it a lot, how he had held her in his arms for hours while she sobbed, and when she finally fell asleep on his cot, how he had wrapped her in his quilt. She'd stayed there with him all night, and even now when she thought about it she felt her cheeks burn. It was a shocking thing for her to do, really, but to this day she wasn't sorry. She was touched.

She threw the scorched window blinds in the trash and bundled up her smelly bedding and a few items of clothing for Ilsa Rowell to launder.

As the days passed, sharing the *Lark* office with Cole continued to make her more and more uneasy. She tried to conduct her newspaper business as usual, monitoring her news beats and writing articles, which Eli set in type twice a week, but things just felt different.

To her surprise, Eli and Noralee Ness were becoming fast friends.

"I like the way Eli smells," the girl confessed. "Like peppermint." Jess had to laugh. The old man devoured bags of peppermint drops from Uncle Charlie's Bakery.

Eli confided that Noralee was "whip smart and has fingers so quick on them fonts I kin hardly keep up with her." Besides, she was a girl, and Eli had always liked females of any age, especially smart ones.

Every afternoon Noralee's long, slim neck bent over her type stick, which brought Eli's avuncular approval. "She's not too purty, but she kin set type faster 'n lightning, and she kin shore make me chuckle."

Cole was growing remote as a fence post. During the day they sashayed around each other in the overcrowded *Lark* office, but Cole began spending most of his time elsewhere. Writing, she supposed. He kept Noralee busy setting type every day after school, and on Saturdays she spent all day cleaning ink off his overworked Ramage press.

Jess's nerves finally snapped when she read the Tuesday edition of the *Lark*. Cole had covered the fire at her office, writing with eloquence about lawlessness and violence. But the headline on the editorial page of his latest issue made her fists clench.

Sheriff Silver Fails
Law Exam

Jessamine crumpled the page into a tight ball and marched down to the restaurant, where she knew Cole was eating breakfast. She tossed the scrunched-up editorial page right in the middle of his scrambled eggs.

"What right do you have spreading lies like this?" she demanded.

He set his coffee cup on its saucer with a crisp clink. "The right of every good newspaperman, or woman, to report the news."

His voice was so calm she felt like screaming. "This isn't news! It's not true."

"It is true, Jess. Sit down and have some coffee."

"How do you know it's true?" She was so furious she grabbed his cup off the saucer and gulped down the contents.

"Telegraph," he said calmly. He signaled Rita to bring another cup. "That's how a journalist keeps up with the news," he said. "I'm in touch with the *Portland Oregonian* office, and they just ran a story on our sheriff."

"That's ridiculous," she replied sharply.

"No, it's not. It's journalism."

"Oh," she breathed. "Oh, poor Jericho."

Cole laughed. "'Poor Jericho' nothing. It won't make a damn bit of difference in the election. At the debate, if you recall, the sheriff made mincemeat of Conway Arbuckle. People are smarter than you think, Jess. It's the *man* they'll be voting for, not the law degree. A law degree isn't a requirement for a district judge, and besides, Jericho can take the exam again in the spring. And besides *that*, Conway Arbuckle is turning out to be a reprehensible skunk."

"Oh," she said again. Cole began pressing the wrinkles out of his rumpled editorial page while Rita splashed coffee into both their cups.

"How are the repairs to your office comin', Miss Jessamine?" the waitress inquired.

"Slowly, Rita. I can hardly wait—" she caught the

fleeting expression that crossed Cole's face "—to, uh, see what it will look like when the carpenter is finished. Mr. Sanders has been very kind in letting me use his press."

"The truth," Cole interjected, "is that Miss Lassiter can hardly wait to get as far away from me as possible. He thumped the page he'd spread out by his plate.

"Cole, that's not true," she blurted out. "It's just that…that…"

The waitress grinned. "I know what you mean, Miss Jessamine. You two ain't exactly like two peas in a pod. More like two Indians tryin' to scalp each other."

"Oh, no," Jessamine protested. "We're…well, we're professional colleagues. Sort of."

"Maybe," Cole muttered.

"Huh! You two can't even agree on an insult." Rita picked up her coffeepot and headed back to the kitchen.

"I—I'm having the upstairs painted a soft rose color," Jess said to change the subject.

"Yeah, I know," Cole said. "I was up there yesterday."

"You were? In my bedroom? Whatever for?"

When he didn't answer she poked her face close to his.

"Why were you in my bedroom?" she repeated.

He wished he'd kept his mouth shut. "Oh, hell,

Jess, I wanted to see where you slept without a lot of smoke in my eyes."

The truth was he'd gone upstairs to her room to see whether her bed was any bigger than his cot. It was, but maybe it didn't matter. Jessamine Lassiter wouldn't be letting him kiss her again if the sky rained daisies all over the rooftops some moonlit night.

She said nothing, but her big green eyes grew even bigger and greener.

"Maybe I'm out of line," he said, his voice quiet, "but I just can't help wondering…" His shirt collar was starting to feel extra tight. "Oh, forget it."

Forget it? Jess knew she would never forget it. Cole had held her all night long after the fire, let her scream and cry and… She bit her lower lip.

"Jess, for God's sake, don't do that."

She blinked at him. She couldn't help biting her lip; she'd done it ever since she was a girl.

She would never know what came over her in the next moment, but she looked right at him, straight into those blue eyes of his, and slowly, carefully, worried her teeth against her lips.

What is wrong with me? She knew how he hated it when she did that. Why was she tormenting him? She felt like a boat that had slipped its mooring and any minute would be sucked into a whirlpool.

I have to stop thinking about Cole Sanders. She couldn't afford to let him distract her from working on her newspaper. If she lost sight of her mission of making a success of the *Sentinel,* if she wavered or let something deter her, the newspaper would suffer. And if that happened, she would lose her livelihood, everything she'd worked for. Even worse, she would be letting down Miles and their father, and his father before him.

Chapter Twelve

Noralee Ness watched Billy Rowell across the street as he started up one side of the boardwalk and down the other, slipping the Saturday edition of the *Sentinel* under doors and through mail slots. Cole studied the girl out of the corner of his eye.

"You in love yet, Noralee?" He couldn't resist asking; he thought she looked more than a little dreamy-eyed of late.

"Huh? No, I'm not. Not with *him,*" she said indignantly. "I don't know who I'm in love with, Mr. Sanders. I haven't met him yet."

"Well, that could slow down a courtship for sure," he quipped.

"Mr. Sanders?"

"Yeah?"

"How long does it take for a girl to grow up?"

Cole frowned. "Grow up? How do you mean, 'grow up'?"

"You know, wear long dresses and lace on her drawers and put her hair up. How long?"

He swallowed. "Depends on the girl."

"Well…me, for instance." She slid off the stool in front of the font case and twirled in front of him. "Me," she repeated.

Hell's bells, she was flat as a frying pan in front and from the back she was straight as a two-by-four. No hips. Not even a hint of a waistline.

"How come you're in such a hurry about growing up, Noralee?"

Her long, narrow face took on a wistful look. "I wanna be just like Miss Jessamine," she said in a faraway voice. "All pretty and proper, just like a lady should be, with petticoats and high-button shoes and—"

She stopped suddenly and looked down at the ink-smudged pinafore she wore over her plain brown poplin dress. "And perfume. Miss Jessamine always smells nice, like violets."

She did smell like violets, Cole acknowledged. A little pointy dart zinged into his chest. She smelled so good it made him ache.

"Yeah," he said at last. "She does smell nice."

"Do you think she'd let me dab some of her perfume behind my ears? That's where ladies wear perfume, you know. And on their throat, so when their skin warms up—"

"Noralee," he interjected, his voice inexplicably

hoarse, "have you finished typesetting that story I gave you this morning?"

She sent him an apologetic look and snatched up her type stick.

For the next hour Cole tried not to think about Jessamine's ears or her throat or her anything else. And he hoped she would not be wearing perfume at the next choir rehearsal. A man could only stand so much.

The next evening was the last rehearsal before the Christmas Eve performance at the church. Cole intercepted Jessamine as she walked from the boardinghouse where she was staying; when she turned toward the church, he gripped her arm.

"Wait," he said. "The rehearsal's not at the church."

"Not at the...? Why not?"

"At the last minute the director decided to hold the performance at the music school. Seems they couldn't move that big grand piano Winifred Dougherty had shipped from St. Louis, so Ike Bruhn donated some planks and got a carpenter to build risers for the back row of singers to stand on."

To be honest, he was relieved. He hated being inside the church, even to sing a beautiful work like the *Messiah*. It reminded him too much of Maryann's funeral.

He took Jessamine's elbow. "Come on, we'll be late."

Inside, the chorus was already warming up, and after ten minutes the director called for silence.

"Ladies, don't forget, no corsets. Now, will the quartet, Mr. Poletti and Mr. Sanders, Mrs. Buchanan and Miss Lassiter, please arrange yourselves in the center?"

Standing next to Jessamine, Cole could sense her nervousness; the music score clutched in her hand fluttered slightly, and she kept biting her lips. Heat flooded his groin.

You damn fool, stop watching.

Halfway through rehearsal of the first chorus, Jess gave a little gasp and swayed toward him. He snaked an arm around her waist to steady her.

"What's wrong?" he whispered.

"Dizzy," she breathed.

"You wearing a corset?"

"Oh." She clapped her hands to her flushed cheeks. "I forgot."

He bent toward her and murmured, "Go take it off before you faint," he murmured. And he'd try not to imagine what she was doing while she was doing it.

The director's arms fell to her sides, and the choir lapsed into silence. "*What* is going on in the back row?" she demanded.

Jessamine froze.

"Miss Lassiter, uh, picked up a stone in her shoe," Cole said smoothly.

"Well, for heaven's sake, go and get rid of it!"

Jessamine blinked. It was the first time she had ever heard Ellie Johnson lose her temper. Now that she thought about it, at the previous rehearsal the marshal's wife had looked quite pale and queasy.

Her journalist's nose twitched. She knew it! Ellie was expecting. Cole would have no clue about the director's coming confinement until the marshal and his wife announced it in the *Sentinel*. That, she gloated, would be a scoop. The *Lark* editor himself wouldn't care, being a man, but her subscribers would relish the story.

Cole gave her a little nudge. Woozy and a bit short of breath because she'd laced the forbidden corset up too tight, she edged through the soprano section and bolted for the anteroom. How embarrassing that he had known what she was wearing underneath her clothes! The man's sharp eyes missed nothing.

And his ears were just as acute. His knack for digging out news stories left her limp with envy. And admiration. If only ladies were allowed in the saloon! That was where the men of the town gathered to talk over events. In the newspaper business it was a great disadvantage to be a woman.

She pressed her lips together. She wasn't beaten yet. She could show Cole Sanders a few things about gathering news in Smoke River. After all, *men* didn't get invited to gossipy ladies tea parties.

She sighed. But men—one man in particular—

did get a woman all flustered just because they—he—touched her.

The following morning Cole and two men from the sawmill hefted Jess's rolltop desk and the apple crates loaded up with her files back across the street into the newly refurbished *Sentinel* office. The place smelled of fresh wood and paint, and her Adams press was disassembled on the floor, awaiting a thorough cleaning, but she was home!

She raced up the stairs to admire the new curtains Verena Forester had sewed for her, a rose-pink calico banded in cream lace. Double-lined. She flung them open to check the view.

Somehow the fact that Cole's bedroom window still faced hers didn't bother her as much now, even though she knew he had spied on her at night. It was hard to stand next to him at rehearsals and sing the beautiful, soaring Handel arias and not feel the pull of an invisible bond between them.

On the last trip from Cole's office, Eli packed up his type sticks and the new font case he'd fashioned out of fruit crates, and Noralee threw her skinny arms around him and snuffled against his shirt.

"I don't want you to go, Mr. Holst. You teach me things, and you make me laugh."

"Aw, honey-girl…" Eli's watery blue eyes looked even more watery. Watching them, Jess felt a lump in her throat the size of a ripe plum.

"You come visit me at the *Sentinel*, why don'tcha?"

Eli said. "On Thursdays I bake cookies for my lunch. You like oatmeal cookies?"

Jess was packing up the last of the newsprint Cole had given her when she caught sight of him standing by his desk with an odd look on his face. Solemnly he extended his hand.

"Good luck over there, Jess. And, Eli, you be sure and keep that revolver handy."

Eli gave him a two-fingered salute, then lumbered out the door and across the street to the *Sentinel*.

Jess extended her hand to Cole, intending to give his a businesslike shake, just as two professional people should. But at the last minute she stretched up and kissed his cheek instead.

"Oh, Jess..." he said. "This has been an experience, hasn't it? Unforgettable. I hope you'll miss me—I mean Noralee and me."

Once Jess had closed the door of her repainted office, it seemed awfully quiet. No metal type clicking. No giggles from Noralee or muttering from Eli's corner. And no sound of Cole's boots tramping about his office.

She'd never thought she would miss it, but she did.

Chapter Thirteen

By Christmas Eve, Jess felt more muddled than ever about Cole Sanders, and when he walked across the street to escort her to the music hall, she found herself excited not only about their performance of the *Messiah* but about the prospect of standing within touching distance of him the entire time.

The evening was clear and frosty, with stars sparkling like diamonds against a blue velvet sky. One streaked toward earth, leaving a silvery path, and she made a wish, then wondered at herself for being so foolish. She had everything she wanted in life, did she not? She had her newspaper back, and even though she supposed that made her attractive to the male population in town, she had never felt even a spark of interest in any potential suitors. Long ago she had decided never to marry. No one but herself would ever have control over her newspaper.

And Cole? What about Cole? He was the only

man she'd ever met who made her breath come short and her heart thrum under her breastbone.

The truth was she didn't know about Cole. She knew only that when she was near him, it made her... well, *want* something.

Cole turned up the collar of his sheepskin jacket against the cold and slipped her hand into his. "Everybody in town will be there tonight," he remarked. "You nervous?"

"Just a bit. Are you?"

He barked out a laugh. "Let's just say this isn't like singing 'Clementine' in the bathtub."

Jess smiled up at him. "Actually, with all those people in the choir singing along with you, this should be a good deal easier than singing 'Clementine.'"

They walked into the recital hall and Jess caught her breath. Every single seat was occupied, and people were standing along the walls and at the back of the room. Suddenly she was more than a bit nervous; a brigade of butterflies fluttered in her stomach.

The choir members warmed up in the small, oak-paneled rehearsal room and then marched two by two into the hall and took their places on the plank risers Ike Bruhn had constructed.

Cole took one look at the sea of faces before them and groaned.

"Take a deep breath," Jessamine whispered.

The director entered, wearing a flared black wool skirt and a lacy white shirtwaist, and took her place. Her husband, Matt Johnson, lounging against the back wall, gave her a thumbs-up.

Ellie turned to the choir, smiled at them and lifted her arms. An expectant hush fell over the audience and Jess heard Cole suck in his breath.

As the first lush opening chord sounded, gasps of surprise erupted from the listeners. The townspeople had never heard anything like a performance of the *Messiah*. She knew they would be entranced. A thrill of anticipation washed over her.

The voices of the choir rose in harmony. "'And the glory, the glory of the Lord…'" An indefinable current of something ran through the singers, and suddenly a soaring rush of emotion took hold of her.

Tears stung her eyes. The music they were making was more than mere notes; it was an expression of human solidarity, of oneness. Jess thought her heart would burst.

How beautiful this is. How extraordinary to be part of this otherworldly creation that transcends all our differences.

When the chorus sang the next anthem, "For unto us a child is born," her entire body began to tremble. Next came the quartet aria, "Behold, and see if there be any sorrow."

Their performance was better than she could have

dreamed, exquisitely nuanced and deeply felt. Prickles began to run up her arms.

Last came the final anthem, the Hallelujah chorus. Cole subtly adjusted his stance so his arm touched hers, and instinctively she moved closer to him. His warmth flooded her entire body. At the final crescendo, Jess felt their individual selves meet and touch, and her chest swelled with a sweet, sharp joy.

When the final chord sounded, the singers stood motionless, without breathing, and the listeners in the room sat in stunned silence.

Ellie's smile was tremulous. *Well done*, she mouthed at them.

And then pandemonium broke out. The audience rose to its feet and shouted and clapped, threw their arms around their neighbors and cheered themselves hoarse.

Cole touched Jess's hand, and she turned to find moisture shining in his eyes. Her heart swam up into her throat.

They walked back to the *Sentinel* building in silence, unwilling to break the spell. At the entrance, Jess spied something leafy and green suspended over the door on a wide red ribbon.

"Mistletoe!" she exclaimed. "Eli must have hung it up after I left."

Cole nodded. "Good man, Eli." He would personally shake the old man's hand the next time he saw him.

Jess sidestepped away from the door, but he grasped her shoulders and jostled her back under the bunch of greenery.

Before she could protest he pulled her into his arms and kissed her.

Mercy, her lips were sweet, like warm honey on a frosty morning. He thought the top of his head would explode, and suddenly alarm bells went off. But after another long, searching kiss, he stopped listening.

"God, Jess," he breathed against her mouth. "What are we doing?"

"No one has ever kissed me like that," she said in a shaky whisper.

"How come?"

She hesitated. "No one has ever kissed me at all, except a boy at school when I was twelve."

"And what happened when he did?"

"My brother Miles tackled him in the schoolyard and bloodied his nose."

Cole laughed and pulled her close, resting his chin against her hair. They stood that way for a long time until he lifted his head and cupped her face between his two hands. Oh, God, he wanted her. He ached with desire.

"Jess?"

"Yes, Cole? My goodness, you look serious. Do you want some of Eli's whiskey?"

He ignored her question. "I guess I'm looking serious because I'm wondering what the hell I'm doing."

"You're kissing me," she said with a soft laugh.

"I thought that was obvious."

"It is, yes."

"Jess…" He hesitated. "Do you want to continue this?" His voice was unsteady.

"How do you mean?"

Dammit, how could he say this? "I think you know how I mean."

She said nothing for so long he thought she hadn't heard him, but he didn't have guts enough to repeat it. What she finally said surprised him.

"Cole, is my bed bigger than yours?"

He jerked upright. "What?"

"I said—"

"I heard what you said. I want to know what you meant by it."

She cleared her throat. "If I remember correctly from the night of the fire, you sleep on a narrow cot."

"Yeah, I do."

She hesitated. "Don't you want to know why I asked?"

"No," he said quietly. "I can guess."

Jess thought she must have gone plain crazy, but she didn't care. Being close to Cole, feeling his arms around her, his mouth on hers, was wonderful beyond her wildest dreams.

God help me, I am in love with this man.

Well, there it was, the thing she'd been trying not to think about ever since the night of the fire. She was falling in love with the editor of her rival newspaper.

"Jess, what are we really talking about here?"

"We're talking about a wonderful, magical thing that is happening on a beautiful night," she said, a smile in her voice.

"You sure you know what you're saying?"

"Hush, Cole. Hush. Let's go inside."

Once inside he stopped her with a hand on her arm. "Look at me, Jess. You're sure about this?"

"I am sure. I'm surprised at myself, but I am sure. More than sure. Why do you ask?"

"Because I want whatever happens between us to matter."

She gazed into his eyes and he felt his head go fuzzy. "It matters, Cole. *You* matter."

He kissed her, then lifted his head with a groan. "I can stop now if you say so. Later, it might not be so easy."

"Don't stop," she breathed. "I don't want you to stop."

He lifted her into his arms and climbed the stairs. In her bedroom he set her on her feet and cupped her face in his hands. "We don't have to go any further, Jess."

"But I want to," she whispered. She laid her hands over his and lifted them to her shoulders, reached both arms about his neck and pulled his head down to hers. "I've never wanted to before, with anyone, but tonight is different."

"What's different about tonight?"

"You. Being with you."

He exhaled heavily. "Oh, Lord, Jess. I don't know how we got here, but I don't want to stop what is happening. I—"

She stopped his words with her lips. He wrapped his arms around her and after a long moment she lifted her head and drew in a shaky breath. "I want to be with you tonight, Cole. All night."

He didn't say anything for a full minute, and then he scooped her up, set her on the edge of the bed, and knelt before her. He slipped both her shoes off, lifted the hem of her skirt and carefully rolled down her stockings. "I've wondered about your feet," he said.

She jerked her bare foot out of his grasp. "My feet! What about them?"

Cole spread his warm fingers over her arch. "They're beautiful. Small and perfect. I thought they would be because your hands are small and fine-boned. I figured your feet would be, too."

He rose and settled himself on the bed beside her.

"Something else I've wondered about," he said, reaching for the top button of her shirtwaist.

She gave a soft laugh. "You mean you thought about my...? Really?"

He made a sound low in his throat. "Sometimes a whole day goes by and all I've done is think about your breasts. Does that shock you?"

"Yes, it's a surprise," she said. "I never realized that a man...well, that his thoughts would..."

"Yeah, his thoughts sure would." He undid the top button, pressed his mouth to her collarbone and undid three more buttons. Then he bent his head, kissed the bare skin above her camisole and slipped his hand inside.

"You smell good," he murmured. "Sweet, like... violets, maybe."

"You smell like woodsmoke. And peppermint."

He didn't answer, just continued unbuttoning her blouse and pressing his lips against the exposed skin. "You like peppermint?"

"I like the way you smell. And I, um, I like what you're doing now."

"Thank God," he breathed. "Because this is only the beginning."

"Oh?" she murmured. "What comes next?"

He thought he heard a smile in her voice, but he wasn't sure. "This." He spread her shirtwaist, slipping it down off her shoulders. "Take it off, Jess."

When she shrugged out of it, he reached for the ribbon of her camisole. "And this."

"Shall I take it off?" she whispered.

"Yeah." He watched as she pulled the loosened garment over her head.

"My God, you are beautiful," he breathed. She sent him a smile, and he rose, stripped off his shirt and winter undershirt, unhooked the leather belt at his waist and toed off his boots. When he looked up she had paused with her hands at the waistband of her skirt.

"Shall I?" she whispered. At his nod, she unhooked the garment and let it slide to the floor.

"Should I take off my petticoats?"

Another nod.

"And then there's my—"

"Jess, stop talking. Just do what I do."

He let his trousers drop to the floor and waited while she untied her petticoat, two petticoats, he noted, a white one with lots of ruffles and another one of soft red flannel.

She looked at him expectantly and he had to laugh. He didn't doubt that she knew how to take off her underclothes; he guessed she was debating whether she *should* or not. Or maybe *when*. He stripped off his drawers, kicked them out of the way and waited.

Her petticoats floated to the floor. Her last undergarment was a pair of the laciest pantalets he'd ever seen, and she hesitated so long he thought he'd go mad. He moved in close, put his hands at her waist and pulled the lacy thing down to her ankles. He heard her suck in her breath.

Gently he pulled her against him and smoothed his hands over her silky rounded bottom. "You are really, really beautiful, Jess."

She pressed her palms against his chest. "You feel strong. Solid."

He laughed quietly. "You feel damn soft." He lifted her off her feet. "Come to bed with me." He walked her backward until her legs touched the bed, tipped her onto the quilt and followed her down.

He grazed one warm, bare breast with his lips, then returned to gently suck the swollen nipple. Her sudden intake of breath told him all he needed to know. He lifted his head to blow gently in her ear, then swirled his tongue into the shell.

Her breathing hitched and she tightened her arms around him. "Oh," she sighed. "Everything you are doing feels wonderful."

He did it again and smiled when he heard her whisper another soft "Oh."

That told him what she liked, and he licked and nuzzled and kissed his way on a leisurely path down to her navel. When he heard her soft moan, he moved farther, until he reached the soft curls at her apex, and he paused.

"Yes," Jess heard herself whisper. "Don't stop."

This is exquisite. Her whole body burned as if it were on fire, and she found herself hungry for his touch, his mouth. His tongue was doing magical things to her aching flesh. She couldn't stop smiling.

Heavens above, I would do anything, anything, *to keep this from ever ending.*

She wanted to entice him, enchant him the way he was enticing her. She wanted all of him.

"Cole?" she murmured.

"Yes," he said. Just that one word, and then he was kissing her everywhere, his mouth hungry, searching, and she was floating up and up to heaven.

He moved over her, nudged her legs apart with his knee. "It might hurt for a minute," he whispered.

"I don't care. I want to be with you."

"I'll make this part fast." He thrust into her and she felt a quick, sharp pain, and then it was over and he was moving deep inside her. It felt wonderful. She felt so intimately connected to him she wondered if she was dreaming.

"Look at me, Jess," he said quietly.

She opened her eyes and met his gaze. They were moving together, even breathing in and out together, and suddenly she felt indescribably happy.

In the next instant something swelled and flowered inside her and she soared away on waves of pleasure.

Oh, this is heaven.

"Jess," Cole said hoarsely. "Oh, God, Jess." His

body went still, and then he was holding her and whispering something and she felt like weeping.

After a long minute he rolled to one side, taking her with him. When he pulled her close his cheeks were wet.

Cole liked Jessamine Lassiter, liked her quiet courage, her curiosity, her quick sense of humor. But he didn't want to *need* her. Or for her to matter too much to him. He liked being with her, sharing scrambled eggs and critiquing each other's newspapers.

He liked being close to her, too. Close enough to touch her, smell her hair. Close enough to kiss her. And he liked kissing her, maybe too much. But he needed to be able to walk away from her.

It would be more than he could stand to lose another woman he loved. After Maryann died he felt shattered inside, as if his bones had splintered and his muscles had dried up and were crumbling into dust. Days passed when he couldn't remember what he'd done; had he eaten? Or spoken to anyone? Had he even left his quiet, empty house?

The weeks had blended into months when he drank too much and thought too much and ached too much, and when the memory of Maryann finally became tolerable, he felt as dead inside as the stuffed eagle mounted over his fireplace mantel.

But he would never forget what it was like to lose

her, and that hell he vowed he would never experience again.

So what are you doing here in Jessamine's bed?

Being hungry for connection. Being full of wanting and grateful for solace.

Being a damn fool.

Chapter Fourteen

Jess opened her eyes to find Cole propped up on one elbow, studying her. "Merry Christmas," he said quietly.

"Merry Christmas." She snuggled her face against his neck, suddenly shy.

"There's something for you in your top desk drawer downstairs."

"Oh!" She hadn't received a present since her brother died. In her bare feet, she padded down the stairs and slid open the center drawer.

Lying on a folded square of yellow calico lay a shiny silver derringer pistol. She smoothed one finger over the polished barrel, then picked it up and weighed it in her hand. It would just fit in her skirt pocket!

Just for pretend, she aimed at the calendar on the wall above Eli's font case, sighted down the barrel and slid her finger onto the trigger. The gun discharged with a deafening roar.

She screamed.

"Jess? You okay?"

"Y-yes."

Then she heard Cole's laughter from upstairs. "Should have told you it's loaded."

Trembling, she stared at the ruined calendar where she had drilled a hole smack in the middle of December. Cole appeared on the staircase, dressed in nothing but a worried frown.

"Jess?"

"I—I'm fine," she said. "But Eli's c-calendar is ruined."

He walked down the stairs and lifted the pistol out of her trembling hand, set it on her desk and wrapped his arms around her. "It's for people like Arbuckle, not target practice," he said with a laugh.

"Of c-course. Thank you, Cole."

"Better come back to bed before the sheriff gets here." He lifted her into his arms and carried her back up the stairs, then curled up under the quilt with her until she stopped shaking. It was wonderful being close to him. She felt more alive than she had ever felt.

Except…

"Cole?" She burrowed her head against his shoulder.

"Yeah?" Cole combed his fingers gently through the dark waves he'd carefully unpinned the night before.

"About last night… I've never done anything like this before."

"I know."

"Does it matter?"

"Sure, it matters. I want it to matter. Did you like it?"

"Oh, yes."

"Then it matters in the right way."

She said nothing for a long time. Then, "You were married before, were you not?"

"Yes. Three years ago."

"Do—do you ever think about her?"

"Yes, I do, Jess. I think about her every day."

Her face changed, but she said nothing.

"I guess when you love someone you always love them," he added. "Even when you—"

He broke off. He wasn't ready to admit what he'd been about to say.

"Even when you what?"

"Jess, it must be obvious how I feel about you. But I have to be honest, I don't ever want to get married again. It hurts too much if something happens."

"You know, I didn't much like you when you first came to Smoke River," she said slowly. "In fact, I hated you. I thought you were nothing but male swagger and know-it-all arrogance."

"And what do you think now?" he asked carefully.

She sighed softly, and her breath tickled his chest hair.

"I think you have a very manly swagger and," she said with a giggle, "that you think you know almost everything. But you are not arrogant. I think you are a good man, Cole. And I understand how you feel about marriage. I feel much the same way. I wouldn't want to give up my independence. Or my newspaper."

He laughed out loud. He couldn't help it. He felt so damn good this morning she could walk all over him with words sharp as railroad spikes and he'd still be smiling into her hair.

And then she surprised him again.

"Cole, I don't feel very experienced. Or very grown-up. You know, very…well, you know what I mean."

He moved his hand to her breast. "You're plenty grown-up, Jess. And experience comes with—" he kissed her erect nipple "—experience."

Jess closed her eyes. Being with this man was glorious beyond imagining.

Much later she drowsily opened her eyes and realized with a jolt that it was no longer morning, it was afternoon. "This is scandalous," she whispered.

"Yeah. Do you like it?"

"Oh, yes. But I'm getting a little hungry."

He sighed. "Then I guess we'll have to get out of bed."

They dressed and walked down to the restaurant. When they ordered, Rita's graying eyebrows rose.

"You want eggs and bacon? Folks, it's three in the afternoon. Where have you—"

The waitress turned a rosy shade of pink and snapped her mouth shut. When her back was turned, Cole lifted Jessamine's hand to his lips.

"Scandalous," he murmured. "In bed all night and half the day."

Jess sucked in a breath and snatched her hand back before Rita saw them. "I—I have an idea for the next issue of the *Sentinel*," she said quickly.

Cole groaned. "Back to rivalry as usual, is it? Okay, what's your idea?"

"Listen to this. The election for district judge is January first. Before then, we could run a series of articles comparing—"

"Nope. I'm not printing one more damn word about Conway Arbuckle."

"As it happens," Jessamine said, her eyes narrowing slightly the way they always did when she thought she was going to scoop him, "I have some interesting new information about Mr. Arbuckle."

Cole stared at the woman he'd taken to bed the night before and then closed his eyes. It was entirely possible, he thought in mounting frustration, that he'd fallen in love with the last woman in the universe he should have.

"Cole?"

He snapped his lids open but couldn't think of one thing to say.

"Cole, I hope that…" She lowered her voice. "That what happened last night and, um, this morning, won't affect our, um, professional relationship."

"It sure as hell will," he murmured. While they stared at each other, Rita tiptoed over with two platters of scrambled eggs and bacon and fluffy sourdough biscuits.

"You two goin' to war again?" she said.

Under the table Cole caught Jessamine's hand in his and squeezed gently. "Type fonts at twenty paces?" he whispered.

Jessamine smiled. Purposely she began to worry her teeth over her bottom lip and watched his eyes darken.

Chapter Fifteen

Cole slapped down the morning edition of Jessamine's *Sentinel* onto his desk, opened it to page two and bolted to his feet.

Conway Arbuckle Fakes
Law Degree
Harvard College reports no attendance record
for Conway Arbuckle!
The candidate for district judge has lied
about his credentials.

"What the—?" This was enough to get her shot or pistol-whipped or worse. "What does she think she's doing?" He crumpled the front page in his fist and headed for the boardwalk.

"Don't yell at her," Noralee called. He slammed the door without answering.

"Jess," he shouted, bursting into her office across

the street. "You can't print this!" He tried not to shout, but his voice rose anyway.

She looked up from her desk, her face unperturbed, and removed the pencil she had clamped between her teeth. "Yes," she said calmly, "I can print it. In fact, I already have. Billy made his rounds an hour ago."

He leaned over her. "I mean you can't print this stuff without proof."

"I have proof," she said, her voice cool. "If you'd bothered to read the entire article, you would know that."

"What proof?" he challenged. "Where'd you dream up this cockamamy story?" By God, Jessamine Lassiter would try the patience of a stone statue. He couldn't begin to imagine about what Arbuckle's response would be.

"The telegraph, of course," she said. "Move over, Cole. You're blocking my light."

"Jess, listen to me."

"Oh, don't get so excited. You should be congratulating me."

"Oh, yeah? What the heck for?"

"For taking a lesson from you. I had Charlie Kincaid at the station house send a telegram to Harvard College. They have no record of Conway Arbuckle's attendance. Ever."

Cole just stared at her. True, this came under the heading of responsible journalism, but it was still dangerous. "Jess, your own brother was shot by an irate reader. Aren't you worried about repercussions?"

"Yes, I am, actually," she admitted. "I—I don't want to get shot or burned out again. But a good newspaper reports the news—you said so yourself. And the telegram I received from Boston yesterday is just that, news."

Ice water pumped into his veins. His belly was already a puddle of mush. "Jess, stop and think a minute."

"Don't yell at me, Cole. I'm nervous enough as it is."

He strode around the corner of her desk, removed the pencil she'd stuck between her teeth and hauled her up into his arms. "I'd die before I'd let anything happen to you, Jess. But how can I keep you safe when you're your own worst enemy?"

"On the contrary," she retorted, her voice rising an octave. "I am not being my own worst enemy. I am being a good friend to my newspaper."

He released a groan of frustration. "I'm going to have to stick to you closer than glue until this election is over. Closer than printer's ink."

"Well, I hardly think—"

"Then don't think," he snapped.

In the far corner, Eli ducked his head and pretended unusual interest in his type stick. "Not much chance of that," he muttered.

Jessamine tightened her lips. "I am surrounded by a couple of overprotective bullies who—"

"No, ya ain't, Jess," Eli sputtered. "Listen to the man and don't interrupt."

Cole shot the old man a grateful look. "Now, either Eli sticks to you twenty-four hours a day for the next..."

He glanced at Eli, who held up the fingers of one gnarled hand. "...five days, or I will. Which is it?"

"Surely you don't mean twenty-four whole hours? Day and...well, night?"

"That's exactly what I mean."

"But that would be—"

"Scandalous," he said softly. "I know that."

"Sensible, though," Eli interjected. He gave Cole a surreptitious thumbs-up and immediately busied himself with his font case.

"I can set up my cot down here," Cole announced.

"For five whole days?" Her voice rose an octave.

"And nights," he growled.

"I—I can't let you—"

"You can't stop me," he interrupted. "Unless you want to shoot me with that new pistol of yours." He sent her a challenging look.

"Well!" she huffed. "You can be sure I am certainly thinking about doing just that."

"Thinking about what? Shooting me or letting me set up a cot in your office?"

Jessamine gritted her teeth. Shooting him had

crossed her mind, but the truth was that the thought of Cole sleeping all night just a staircase away from her made her feel hot and cold all over.

Mostly hot.

What was she thinking? She could not possibly let him stay here at night. On the other hand, she quailed at the thought of being threatened or attacked.

"What will people think?"

"Nuthin'," Eli volunteered. "Cole kin come on over here after ever'body in town's gone to bed, and I ain't gonna say a word."

"Case closed," Cole announced. "Now, about that telegram you sent to Harvard."

Jess bit her lip. "What about it?"

"Hell, I wish you'd never sent it."

"It's too late. I did send it, and I received an answer. I wanted to expose Conway Arbuckle. And," she added, "I wanted to pay him back for having my office torched. Sheriff Silver even said he suspected Arbuckle was behind it."

"Jess, revenge has no place in good journalism. You have to have proof to accuse Arbuckle of setting that fire. Even if it's plain to you and me that he did it to get back at you for what you printed about him, the sheriff can't arrest him without proof. And Jericho didn't find anything concrete that ties him to the fire."

"Oh, I know that. But it still galls me that Arbuckle did what he did and he's not behind bars."

Cole propped his hands on his hips. "You haven't read the lead article in Friday's *Lark*, have you?"

"Well, no, I haven't. What does it say?"

"You'll read it on Friday. In the meantime…"

Eli chuckled. "In the meantime, Cole, whyn'tcha go get yer cot and set it up tonight?"

"Good thinking, Eli. Every newspaper needs a man like you."

"Aw, shucks, Cole. Don't take no thought a'tall to care about Miss Jessamine, now, do it?"

Cole gritted his teeth and didn't answer.

Jessamine closed her mouth and began counting the hours until dark when Cole would be there.

He could hear Jessamine moving around upstairs, making little rustling noises and humming snatches of melodies he couldn't identify. Her footsteps made the floor creak, but he knew she was barefoot because there was no other sound.

Was she glad he was here, tossing on his narrow cot a floor below her? He wondered suddenly where she'd stashed her new derringer—in her desk drawer? Under her pillow? Now that he thought about it, under her pillow wouldn't be such a smart idea. If he climbed the stairs, she might shoot him.

He folded his arms under his head and wondered if Eli would mind if he drank some of the whiskey he kept stashed under the cabinet. He felt more than a little unhinged, partly because he was sleeping here, so close to Jess, but even more because he couldn't *not* sleep here. His gut tightened at the thought of Arbuckle sneaking into the premises at night. He kept listening for footsteps.

There was something else, too. He was more than a little puzzled about why she had allowed them only one night of making love together.

Because she's a real lady, and a man doesn't dally with a real lady.

That night with Jess had been the best Christmas present he'd ever received, and that included nights with his wife, back in Kansas. He didn't feel disloyal, exactly. He just felt hot and kind of squashed-up inside when he thought of Jess or heard her voice or touched her. Even accidentally grazing her arm under those buttoned-up long-sleeved shirtwaists proper ladies wore made him need to shift his jeans around some.

He flopped over onto his other side. He'd locked the front door and hadn't lit a lamp; no one out walking at night would know that he was camped out in her office.

Suddenly he spied something out the front window, a shadowy figure across the way, lounging under the overhang of the *Lark* office.

He sat up.

He hoped to hell Jess had not lit the lamp upstairs. After a few minutes the figure moved on down the street and Cole lay down again. Maybe someone had just stopped to roll a cigarette. Lord, he was jumpy as a green mustang.

He had just closed his eyes a second time when he heard the faint *scrick* of the doorknob turning. Very slowly he slid off the cot and reached underneath for his Winchester.

He waited. After a long moment he heard an odd noise, like someone scratching a hairpin into the lock. He bolted off the cot and crept to the front window for a closer look. Sure enough, a dark figure was bent over the doorknob.

Cole stood without moving, weighing the situation and his options. He could fire at the man out the front window, scare him off, maybe even wing him. But that would scare the heck out of Jess, and then he'd never know who the man was.

Or he could position himself behind the door and wait until the lock yielded, then confront whoever it was.

No, he couldn't. If the fellow was armed, there might be gunplay, and Jess could get hurt.

He decided to make a noise and startle the man into leaving. Quietly he backed away from the window, reached for the rollup top on Jess's desk and slid it up and down with a hard rattle and snap.

Footsteps pounded down the boardwalk. Cole strained his ears listening for a horse, but he heard nothing more. So the man was on foot, not horseback. And that suggested it was someone from town.

Quietly Cole unbolted the lock and cracked open the door.

He could hear men's laughter from the saloon down the street, the snip and twitter of night birds, even the lonely whistle of a train somewhere. Night sounds.

But no horses' hooves. No gunfire. Nothing but the ominous quiet of a dark street in the middle of the night.

He shut the door, locked and bolted it, slid his rifle back under the cot and lay down on top of the quilt. The rhythmic thump-thump he heard was his own heartbeat, and he smiled wryly into the dark and wondered how many hours until dawn.

First thing tomorrow he'd pay another visit to Sheriff Jericho Silver.

Jessamine bent over the proofs Eli had run off, working her teeth into her pencil. She had a bad feeling about this election. She believed Jericho Silver could win a majority of the votes, but she could not help wondering what Conway Arbuckle would do if he lost the race. She hadn't seen the man lately, at the hotel or anywhere else, and Rosie Greywolf reported that he had not visited his "other wife" all week.

Rosie kept her sharp eye on town happenings and she missed nothing. Usually. But the Indian woman did live in a cabin half a mile outside town, so she couldn't see everything that went on twenty-four hours a day.

Tomorrow the townspeople would vote, along with residents of Gillette Springs, which would fall under the new judge's jurisdiction. No doubt Arbuckle was out this very minute canvassing votes in that community.

She was so worked up that when she inadvertently smeared the ink on her proof copy she unexpectedly burst into tears, then went ahead and let herself have a good cry. She couldn't imagine what was wrong with her. Nerves, probably. She hadn't been sleeping much at night, knowing Cole lay just twelve steps away.

She liked having him near. Liked feeling protected. But still… Oh, she felt all mixed up inside. She couldn't just tiptoe down the stairs and crawl into his bed at night. He still had his memories of his wife, and she… Well, it wouldn't be fair to grow too close to him, since there was really no future in it for either of them. Yes, she had fallen in love with him, and maybe he even loved her, but…it was not enough.

Later, while Eli cranked off copies of the *Sentinel*'s morning edition, she tried to talk sense to herself. The election would be over soon and things would get back to normal. She would report on Mrs. Hinksley's whist party and the latest engagement announcement and birthday celebration. And of course

FREE Merchandise is 'in the Cards' for you!

Dear Reader,

We're giving away FREE MERCHANDISE!

Seriously, we'd like to reward you for reading this novel by giving you **FREE MERCHANDISE** worth over **$20** retail. And no purchase is necessary!

It's easy! All you have to do is look inside for your Free Merchandise Voucher. Return the Voucher promptly...and we'll send you valuable Free Merchandise!

Thanks again for reading one of our novels—and enjoy your Free Merchandise with our compliments!

Pam Powers

Pam Powers

P.S. Look inside to see what Free Merchandise is **"in the cards"** for you!

W

e'd like to send you two free books like the one you are enjoying now. Your two books have a combined price of over $10 retail, but they are yours to keep absolutely FREE! We'll even send you 2 wonderful surprise gifts. You can't lose!

REMEMBER: Your Free Merchandise, consisting of **2 Free Books** and **2 Free Gifts**, is worth over $20 retail! No purchase is necessary, so please send for your Free Merchandise today.

Get TWO FREE GIFTS!
We'll also send you 2 wonderful FREE GIFTS (worth about $10 retail), in addition to your 2 Free books!

Visit us at:
www.ReaderService.com

Books received may not be as shown.

YOUR FREE MERCHANDISE INCLUDES...

2 FREE Books **AND** 2 FREE Mystery Gifts

FREE MERCHANDISE VOUCHER

❏ Please send my Free Merchandise, consisting of
2 Free Books and **2 Free Mystery Gifts**.
I understand that I am under no obligation to buy
anything, as explained on the back of this card.

246/349 HDL GKA4

Please Print

FIRST NAME

LAST NAME

ADDRESS

APT.#   CITY

STATE/PROV.   ZIP/POSTAL CODE

NO PURCHASE NECESSARY!

HH-516-FMH16

the news about the railroad strike in the East and where General Custer would next confront the Sioux.

But she felt uneasy, as if something terrible was about to happen. How she wished life could be the way it was before.

But that was before Cole had come to Smoke River, and she did not wish for that.

She put on a determined smile for Eli's benefit, retrieved her notebook, sharpened a fresh pencil and prepared to leave the office to check her news beats.

Chapter Sixteen

Cole looked up to find young Teddy MacAllister bending over his shoulder, his russet eyebrows pulled down into a frown. "Mr. Sanders?"

"Yes, what is it, son?"

"I—I got a suggestion for you. 'Bout Miss Jessamine. An' I brought you something to help."

"What about Miss Jessamine, Ted? Nothing wrong with her printing press, is there? She got enough ink?"

"Nah, nuthin' like that. Just now she was helping me load up the *Sentinel* copies to distribute, and she was sorta snuffly, like she'd been cryin'."

Cole surveyed the boy in silence. Jess never cried, except for the night her newspaper was firebombed. His neck prickled.

"I'll just mosey on over there and check on her," he said.

Teddy shoved a small cardboard box onto Cole's

desk. "This is for you, to take to Miss Jessamine. Like I told ya, before, 'member?"

Inside the box was a collection of dried grasshoppers. "Bugs," Teddy explained. "It's what I give to Manette, an' I thought it'd help with Miss Jessamine."

Cole couldn't laugh in front of the boy, but he bit the inside of his lower lip so hard he tasted blood. "Mighty thoughtful of you, Ted. I'll see it gets delivered, for sure."

The boy grinned and raced out to mount his mare, his saddlebags laden with newspapers. Smiling, Cole watched him go larruping down the street, and then he sobered.

Jessamine was crying? Why?

He was across the street in twenty seconds. "Eli, where's Jess?"

The old man looked up from the sandwiches spread out on his workbench. "Dunno. At the restaurant, mebbe. It's past lunchtime."

When Cole entered the restaurant, Rita glanced up, tipped her head toward the table in the far corner and headed for the coffeepot. He moved forward and turned the chair that was next to Jessamine backward then straddled it. "What's up?"

"Nothing, Cole. Why? My goodness, you look awful. Are you getting enough sleep at night?"

"Nope. But let's discuss that later. Teddy said you've been crying."

Her red-rimmed eyes widened. "Teddy? Well, yes, I have, but how would he know that?"

"He said you were 'snuffly' when you were loading up the newspapers. What's wrong, Jess?"

"Oh, I— It's nothing, really."

Rita marched over and stood at his elbow, notepad poised. "You eatin' or just jawin'?"

"Coffee," he said.

"Got a nice chicken-fried steak on the menu."

"Just coffee."

"Fresh apple pie, too," the waitress persisted.

"Just one cup of coffee, Rita," he said, his voice tightening. "Please."

Rita went back to the kitchen, muttering under her breath. "Stubborn? Never seen two such stubborn..."

Cole hitched his chair closer. "Jess, has something happened? Somebody threaten you?"

She shook her head.

He leaned in closer. "Are you... Oh, my God, are you pregnant?"

She clapped her hand to her mouth to stifle a shocked laugh, then shook her head again. "No, I am not." Then her eyes filled with tears.

"Jess?"

"It's this dratted election. The waiting. The rumors. The—"

"You're not pregnant," Cole breathed. Hell's bells, he was halfway disappointed. "Teddy MacAllister was worried about you. He brought over a special gift for me to give you."

She smiled. "Oh, that's nice. What is it?"

"A box of bugs."

"Bugs!"

"Grasshoppers. Seems they're a love offering he takes to Jeanne and Wash Halliday's daughter, Manette."

"Bugs," she repeated. "Oh, how sweet."

"You'd like a box of grasshoppers?"

She laughed. Thank God. Her eyes looked dry and so green and clear he wanted to swim around in them.

"The election is tomorrow," he reminded her. "Voting box will be at Ness's Mercantile. Sit with me?"

"I suppose we should. Marshal Johnson is the official ballot monitor, but he'll need two witnesses."

"I'm composing a piece about Arbuckle for when he concedes," he said dryly.

"I'm writing a story based on Jericho's acceptance speech."

"Should boost both our subscriptions," Cole ventured.

"Again," she added. "After this we'll need a new controversy to keep sales booming."

Cole laughed. "Think maybe we can find something new to argue about?"

But she isn't pregnant. He guessed maybe they

would disagree about whether that was a relief or a disappointment.

"For pity's sake, Cole, why are you looking at me like that?"

"Like what?"

"Like I have strawberries growing out of my ears."

He started to laugh and then choked it off. "I guess because in a lot of ways you're beginning to scare me, Jess."

Her teacup jiggled, and she carefully disengaged her finger from the delicate curved handle. "I cannot imagine why *I* should scare *you*. You're the one sleeping with a rifle under your bed. Oh, yes, I know it's there. Eli told me."

"Damn that old man!"

"Eli cares about me, Cole. He tries his best to watch over me."

"Eli can't protect you. I doubt he can see two yards in front of his nose."

She bit her lip and he suppressed a groan. He knew she wasn't teasing him this time; she was worried about something. He just didn't know what. Her fond but feeble typesetter? Her newspaper circulation? *His* newspaper circulation?

Or was it *him* she was worried about?

He didn't like it when a woman worried over him. It distracted her, made her careless about things that could harm her.

He reached for the coffee mug in front of him and closed his fingers around it until his knuckles whitened. Maryann had worried about him. She hadn't liked him working late at the newspaper office, and she hadn't wanted him to continue publishing articles denouncing slavery and accusing Quantrill of the mayhem and violence he had brought to an already divided Kansas.

Cole hadn't listened to her fears, and he would regret it until the day he died. One night, while his attention had been focused on his press run, someone set fire to his house. He had been two blocks away when he saw the flickering glow in the sky.

He'd started to run.

The house had been an inferno. He'd seen Maryann in the window on the second floor, and he'd shouted for her to jump. Just as she'd climbed out onto the sill, the blazing roof had caved in on her.

He could hear her screaming, and then there had been nothing but the roar of the flames.

Even now he could hear her screaming. He shuddered at the memory and jerked himself back to the present. Sweat beaded on his face. God in heaven, he hated remembering.

He hated the fear that pooled in his belly, cold and sour; and he knew he would be a coward all his life because he couldn't let it go, couldn't move forward. His wife had been snatched from him, and he didn't want another.

He didn't like what that said about him, but he knew he was no good for Jess. She deserved better. She deserved a man who was willing to risk everything for her.

Chapter Seventeen

Election day dawned cold and crisp, the sky blue as forget-me-nots and so clear and cloudless it looked as if it had been painted. At the mercantile, Jess perched on a stool next to Cole and huddled close to the fire in the potbellied stove.

Federal Marshal Matt Johnson strode up and down between the aisles of men's shirts and canning supplies, rubbing his hands together and flexing his fingers. He stopped at the counter and purchased a box of cartridges for the revolver strapped around his hips.

Jess shivered. The marshal was here to oversee the election proceedings and make sure everything stayed peaceful. Cole tipped his hat back and settled himself next to the oversize molasses tin serving as the ballot box. A slit had been cut in the top for the paper ballots, printed up that morning on Cole's Ramage press. The ink was barely dry.

All day long they sat there, watching as people folded and dropped their ballots in the box, then hung around the warm stove exchanging news. The mercantile owner supplied sandwiches and coffee, but the hours dragged. Toward the end of the day, Jess could barely stop yawning.

Late that night they helped to tally the ballots. Jericho Silver won, garnering nine hundred and ninety-six votes to Conway Arbuckle's one hundred and eight, but even so, Jessamine could not shake the feeling that something was wrong. Whether it was the unusually still night or the absence of a moon or the decisive way mercantile owner Carl Ness had packed up his molasses tin ballot box and shooed the marshal and Cole and herself out of his store, she couldn't say.

What she could say without a flicker of doubt was that her nose for news hadn't stopped twitching since yesterday afternoon.

At midnight, Cole walked her back to the *Sentinel* office.

"Long day," he said, his voice noncommittal.

"I know you've already been working a story about Arbuckle's defeat."

"Yeah, I have my story half-written. I'll just step over to my office, finish it up and make sure it's sitting where Noralee can find it in the morning. Lock your door, Jess. I'll use the extra key Eli gave me when I come back over."

"It's a good thing that girl worships you, Cole. You work her to death."

"No, I don't. She likes setting type. Wouldn't be a bit surprised if she ended up running her own newspaper someday."

Jessamine sighed. "Funny how the bug bites you, isn't it? Until Miles was killed, I never thought I'd run a newspaper, either."

Cole touched her shoulder briefly and stepped out onto the boardwalk. He waited to hear her lock click, then went across the street to the *Lark* office.

Once inside, he swept up his handwritten pages. He had just turned toward Noralee's array of type fonts when someone grabbed him from behind and pinned his arms. He drove his elbow backward into the fleshy part of a man's belly and followed it up with a kick to his shin.

Then someone slapped a wadded-up cloth over his nose and mouth. It smelled odd, kinda sweet, but before he could rip it away, everything went black.

Jessamine was up at dawn, hoping to catch Cole before he folded up his cot. All night she'd thought about an idea for a feature, and she hurried down the stairs to tell him.

His cot was still there, the quilt neatly folded on top. But it looked as if his bed hadn't been slept in, and that was odd. Even more odd was the fact that he'd left it out in plain sight. She'd have to speak to him about that before he went to breakfast.

At ten o'clock Noralee Ness stepped into the *Sentinel* office, her thin arms clasped across her middle. "Have you seen Mr. Sanders this morning?"

Jess removed the pencil between her teeth. "He's probably at breakfast, Noralee. We were up late last night, counting the ballots."

"He's not at the restaurant, Miss Jessamine. I checked. And Rita said she hasn't seen him all morning."

A jolt of fear went up Jess's spine. "Eli?" she called over her shoulder.

"I ain't seen him, neither, Jess. Musta got up real early, 'cause his cot—" He broke off with a glance at Noralee's worried face.

The girl turned puzzled brown eyes on Jess. "He was going to leave me a story to typeset this morning, about the election," Noralee said. "But I found the pages scattered all over the floor. Should I pick them up and set the story up anyway?"

Eli and Jessamine stared at each other for a long minute.

"I'll go check the Golden Partridge, Jess," Eli said. "See if he's celebratin' or news-gatherin' or…"

"Seems awful funny," Noralee said with a catch in her voice. "Mr. Sanders, he always does what he says he's going to do. He said he'd have a story for me to work on this morning, and now I don't know what to do."

Jessamine rose to her feet, her throat dry and her heart beginning to pound under her ruffled white shirtwaist. "I'm going over to the livery stable, Eli. Maybe he's out riding that Arabian of his."

"But Miss Jessamine," Noralee protested, "why would he be riding around on his horse today instead of writing his news stories? The *Lark*'s supposed to come out tomorrow morning."

A shard of ice dropped into Jessamine's stomach. She skipped the livery stable and instead went straight to the sheriff's office. After a tense ten minutes of wrapping her shaking hands around a cup of coffee, the deputy sheriff strode in and slapped his hat on the sheriff's paper-strewn desk.

"His horse is there, all right, Sheriff. Hasn't been ridden."

"Sandy," the sheriff ordered. "Ride out to Wash Halliday's place. Tell him I need him. Tell him to meet me at Marshal Johnson's."

Jericho began checking his revolvers and Jess jumped to her feet. "What is it? What has happened?"

A strained expression crossed the sheriff's tanned face. "There's no easy way to put this, Miss Jessamine. Looks like Cole's been kidnapped."

Chapter Eighteen

Cole found himself tied belly-down on the back of a horse, his head aching as if a cannon had gone off inside his skull. He groaned and someone pulled the animal to a stop.

"Awake, are ya?" Well, I reckon ya kin sit up. We'll make better time that way."

Someone jerked him off the horse, and then the hard barrel of a gun prodded him in the back. "Mount up," the voice ordered. A swarthy man lashed his hands to the saddle horn, and another, taller man stepped over and slapped the animal's rump so it jolted forward.

Three men. Cole couldn't be sure if they were the same three he'd seen in the saloon the night of the fire, but it seemed likely. He'd thought they were all in jail.

Guess not. Or maybe Jericho had released them for lack of concrete evidence. Or maybe they had nothing to do with Arbuckle or the fire at Jess's newspaper office. He hated not knowing.

He studied the countryside around him. Mostly scrub with a copse of cottonwoods here and there. Didn't recognize it from his newspaper route or from any of his journeys around the valley on horseback. From the angle of the sun, he guessed they were heading east, into the badlands.

They rode for about three hours, then stopped to water the horses. Someone shoved a rusty canteen at him, but with his hands tied, he couldn't grasp it.

A few words of Spanish from one of the men, the fat, swarthy one, and the rope around Cole's hands was loosened. He gulped the liquid greedily, but before he handed back the canteen he managed to slip a scrap of paper out of his shirt pocket, an extra ballot from last night's election.

Hiding his motions, he tore it into tiny pieces, and when nobody was watching, he let one flutter to the ground. The rest he stuffed up his shirtsleeve. Just in time. Fat Man stomped over and retied his hands.

Who were these guys? Did they work for Arbuckle? He knew he was a thorn in the man's side because of his recent editorials. Cole just never thought he'd go this far.

He hoped to hell someone had noticed he wasn't at the *Lark* office this morning. He hoped someone would notify the sheriff, and he prayed that

Jericho Silver was as good a tracker as everybody said he was.

Another three hours passed. His throat was parched and he felt dizzy with hunger. Without his hat, the sun was frying his brains. He closed his eyes and tried to think.

Chances were he wasn't going to survive this. He'd bet whoever these guys were they had orders to take him out to some remote canyon and kill him, probably because of something he'd printed in his newspaper. Somehow he didn't mind the idea of dying; what he hated was the thought of never seeing Jess again, never hearing her laugh or watching her lips turn rosy when she caught them between her teeth.

He closed his eyes. He'd known for some while he'd have a hard time not being around her. It had never occurred to him he wouldn't have a chance to say goodbye.

Each time they stopped to water the horses, Cole managed to let another bit of paper drop unnoticed onto the ground. He'd give anything for a pencil so he could scratch a message to Jess.

But what message?

He thought of a thousand things he'd give his right arm to tell her. Right at the top of the list was *I love you*. Then he'd tell her to take over the *Lark*. Or maybe she'd know instinctively that he would want her to have it.

He gritted his teeth at the thought he might never see her again, and his throat closed into a tight knot.

Another stop to rest the horses and another slip of paper fluttered out of his sleeve. By now they were picking their way uphill, into a rocky canyon. Even if he could twist around far enough to deck one of them, or grab him to use as a hostage, he knew the other two would gun him down before he could take a breath.

Arbuckle would burn in hell for this. And if he laid a hand on Jess...

Sweat slicked the back of Cole's neck. He couldn't help her. He couldn't do a damn thing to change the outcome of this day. He'd never felt more helpless in his life.

The wind knifed through him, and he tried to pray.

Jessamine sat Noralee down and stuffed a type stick into her hand. "I will finish Cole's articles. You set the type. We're going to get his Friday edition of the *Lark* out on time."

Eli patted the girl's narrow shoulder with a gnarled, ink-stained hand. "Don't you fret none, Noralee. Sheriff Silver and the marshal and Wash Halliday rode out an hour ago, and there's no better trackers than them three. They'll bring Cole back."

Jess tried hard to believe the old man, tried not to think about where Cole might be or what he was enduring. It squeezed all the air out of her lungs and made her vision blur. After another hour at his desk, she jerked to her feet and then immediately sat back down.

She felt like screaming, but she forced her pencil back and forth over the pad in front of her and tried to think like Cole. How would he phrase this sentence? What emphasis would he want?

"I'm going over to the Golden Partridge," she announced suddenly. "That was part of Cole's news beat, and I'm going to cover it for him."

"Jess, you cain't—"

"Oh, yes, I can, Eli. Just you watch me." She'd be darned if she would let Cole's newspaper miss a deadline. She slipped her notepad into her skirt pocket, along with the derringer Cole had given her, marched down the sidewalk to the saloon and pushed her way through the batwing doors.

Her first step inside the dim saloon was greeted with dead silence. Then a male voice yelled, "Hey, you can't come in here! No ladies allowed."

"Maybe I'm not a lady," Jess shot back. "You ever think of that?"

She advanced to the bar and caught the bartender's eye. "I'll have a cup of hot tea."

"He's right, Miss Jessamine," he said. "Women aren't allowed in here."

"Listen, Mr. O'Reilly." She lowered her voice and leaned across the gleaming mahogany bar toward him. "Something has happened to Cole Sanders. I'm here to find out any information you might have, and I'm not leaving until I have it."

The barkeep shifted his rotund body toward her. "Miss Jessamine, you look like you need a shot of something a whole lot stronger than tea."

"I do, and that is a fact. But not until I find out what I want to know. The sheriff and Marshal Johnson have ridden out, along with Wash Halliday. Have you any idea who they're chasing?"

"Wish I did, Miss Jessamine. Haven't been any strangers in town since the night your office burned, and I heard later that Sheriff Silver arrested some men, but he wasn't sure they were the ones that did it."

"Maybe there are more? Have you any idea who they are? Who they work for?" This last was a shot in the dark. She'd bet her mother's emerald brooch Conway Arbuckle was involved, but it wouldn't hurt to fish.

The bartender shrugged.

"Tom," she whispered. "Help me. Please."

O'Reilly grabbed a bottle and a shot glass, filled it and set it in front of her. "Arbuckle's holed up at Lucy's place, just outside town. You wouldn't know it, 'cause it's a…well, a place you wouldn't know. Anyway, I hear he's madder'n a wet hornet about losing the election. Might be he blames Cole."

Jess downed the whiskey in one gulp and choked as the fiery liquor burned its way down her throat.

"Thanks, Tom," she rasped. "Put the drink on Cole's tab."

Arbuckle. That snake.

Back out on the boardwalk, she headed for Lucy's place. Oh, yes, she knew where it was. Rosie Greywolf had told her.

The house sat on a back street lined with maple trees. It was painted white with dark blue trim, but it looked run-down. The front porch planks were beginning to warp, and what had once been a flower garden looked withered and so bedraggled she wished she had a bucket of water to dump on the struggling plants.

She walked up onto the porch, took a steadying breath and pounded her fist on the door. No answer. She pounded again and kept pounding until a white-faced woman with frizzy red hair yanked it open. She was dressed only in a dirty chemise and a torn petticoat.

The woman took one look at Jessamine and retreated into the interior of the house. Arbuckle's "other wife," no doubt. She looked terrified.

Jessamine clenched her fists and stepped forward. "Arbuckle?" she shouted.

"Ah, the nosy newspaper lady," a strident voice returned from somewhere. "Go away."

"I'm not going away until you talk to me." She

stepped inside, noting the drawn curtains and the clothing strewn over a dingy sofa in the front parlor. She guessed the snake was packing to leave.

"Arbuckle, I want to talk to you!"

Something rustled from behind the tall wardrobe against the far wall, and that told Jess where he was. She drew out her pistol, cocked it and stepped around the corner of the tall piece of furniture.

Arbuckle's head jerked up and he glared at her with rheumy eyes.

Jess lifted the pistol and aimed it at his chest. "You are a lying, cheating rabbit of a man, and if you don't tell me where Cole Sanders is, I'll kill you."

"Oh, God, don't shoot!" He peered at her face. "Nah, you wouldn't do that," he drawled. "Would you?"

"Oh, no? Try me." She took a step closer and watched his bravado crumble. His thick arms lifted into the air.

"Where is Cole Sanders?"

"I dunno."

"You lying skunk, tell me!"

"I would if I could, Miss Lassiter. But, God's truth, I don't know."

"I don't believe you."

"You gotta believe me," he whined. "Sure, I hired a couple of men to kidnap him, but—"

"The same men you hired to torch my office?" She wondered why her voice wasn't shaky, or why the hand gripping her derringer was steady. Maybe it was the whiskey she'd downed at the Golden Partridge.

"Well, it might be," Arbuckle conceded. "Could be it was the same fellas. Isn't gonna help knowing that now, is it?"

"It might."

"Good God, Miss Lassiter, could you lower your weapon?"

"No, I could not. Now tell me the truth."

Arbuckle looked right, and then left, over his shoulder, as if he was afraid of being overheard. "Well, after the election, I told some men to take Sanders out and… Miss Lassiter, for the love of God, you aren't gonna shoot me, are you?"

"That depends," she replied. "Keep talking."

"Don't kill me," he pleaded. "I'll tell you. I'll do anything you say."

"Then march, Mr. Arbuckle. Out of this house and up the street to the jail. I'll be right behind you with my pistol aimed at your cowardly back."

"You've got no right to have me arrested!"

"Oh, yes, I do. I think you had my newspaper office burned. And if Cole Sanders is found—" she could scarcely bear to say the word "—dead, you will be held as an accessory to murder. Now march!"

Arbuckle stumbled along the street, Jessamine a pace behind him, her pistol steady and her stride determined. Townspeople they met along the way shrank into storefronts and doorways as they passed.

At the jail, the deputy leaped up from the paper-littered desk. "Miss Jessamine?"

"Sandy, lock up Mr. Arbuckle until they find Cole Sanders. And if they don't find him…" Her voice choked off. "Then throw away the key."

Sandy snapped a pair of handcuffs onto Arbuckle's thick wrists and led him away. When she heard the jail-cell door clang shut, she slipped the derringer's safety on, stowed the weapon in her skirt pocket and fainted dead away.

Federal Marshal Matt Johnson pointed to another scrap of white paper that had blown up against a spiky coyote bush. "Been following this trail for half a day, Jericho. You got a plan?"

"Yeah. Wait till dark."

"He might be dead by then. Chances are these men are wanted in half a dozen territories. They might not wait."

"They'll wait."

"What makes you so sure?"

"I figure they haven't been paid yet," the sheriff said. "So they'll keep Cole alive until whoever hired them arrives with the money."

"Maybe," the marshal said, doubt coloring his voice.

Wash Halliday kicked at a stone. "And maybe not."

Without speaking, the three men remounted and rode another mile.

"Be dark in an hour," Matt finally said.

"Yeah," Jericho agreed, eyeing the position of the sun. "Let's split up. Surround that canyon up yonder and wait."

"You figure it's Arbuckle, don't you, Jericho?"

"I do. And in exactly fifteen days I'll be in a position to deal out some justice."

"What about now?" Wash wondered aloud.

"Now I'm still the sheriff. Let's dismount and start crawling."

Chapter Nineteen

Cole licked his chapped lips and wondered why his momma had never taught him any prayers. Even a little short one would do right about now.

He'd spent the last two nights tied to a pine tree while the three men who'd taken him slurped whiskey and took turns guarding him. None too gently. The one he'd nicknamed Swarthy liked to kick his leg to keep him awake. The bastard gave an ugly laugh when he did it, and Cole tried to shut down his hearing.

He didn't know how much longer he could go without passing out from thirst or getting himself shot trying to escape. *Dear God in heaven, don't let the end be so bloody it'll be hard for Jess to see my body.*

His eyes began to burn and he closed them tight. He could see Jessamine bent over the desk in the *Sentinel* office, scribbling away with that tooth-marked pencil she always used; see her sitting across the table from him at the restaurant, calmly drinking tea and biting her lower lip while he fought his need to climb over the platters of scrambled eggs and kiss her silly.

And that night in her upstairs room when she touched him for the first time...

Shoot. As exhausted and hungry as he was, he felt his groin tighten.

Someone jerked the rope that bound his wrists to the saddle horn. "What're ya smilin' about, Sanders?"

"None of your business," Cole bit back.

"Oh, ho," the oily voice said. "Think you're gonna see her again, huh?"

Cole kept his mouth shut. He'd bet his last dollar he wouldn't see Jess again. The thought made his throat ache.

"Well, ya kin fergit that, mister. You ain't never gonna see her, or anybody else, in that stinkin' town."

That made him mad. "Yeah? Who says so?"

"Arbuckle, fer one," the voice beside him said. "He's payin' us."

"Yeah? Who else?" *Keep him talking. He needed names.*

"Shut him up, Jim," the swarthy man on the lead horse snarled.

Cole noted that one of the men hadn't said a word. He heard the whisper of metal against leather and knew someone had just drawn a gun. He swore under his breath. Dammit, he wasn't going out without a fight.

He kicked his mount hard. The animal lurched ahead, and Cole swung his leg out and drove the toe of his boot into the belly of the horse beside his. The mare shied and Swarthy hauled on the reins. The horse reared, and the man grabbed for the pommel.

"You're gonna pay for that, Sanders."

"How much do you want? I'll double whatever Arbuckle's paying you."

There was a long silence, and then the tall man spoke. "You hear that, Jim? He says he'll double our take."

"He ain't gonna live long enough to pay us anything." He spurred ahead into a narrow box canyon clotted with salal and thick scrub. Plenty of brush thick enough to hide a body.

Cole swallowed.

Then out of the corner of his eye he saw a branch twitch. Purposefully he looked away and kept his face impassive. Might have been nothing but a jackrabbit or a deer. He listened hard, but he could hear nothing but the soft sighing of the wind in the fir branches overhead.

Behind him "Jim" lashed the rump of Cole's horse with his quirt. "Hurry up, newsman. We ain't got all day."

The horse jolted forward. Cole studied the vegetation beside the narrow, unused trail for any sign that he wasn't alone, but he saw nothing.

"Hey!" Swarthy yelled. "Slow that nag down."

"If you untie my hands, I could control her better," Cole said.

"Fat chance, Sanders. Shut up and keep ridin'."

Cole kept his head down. From long years as a newspaper reporter, he'd learned to pay attention to the sixth sense he often felt inside that told him something logic had not revealed. Jess would call it her "nose for news." Right now his nose was telling him he and the three men pushing him along the trail weren't the only ones in this tangle of trees and undergrowth.

They rode deeper into the canyon, and suddenly Cole knew how it would end. The men would kill him, kick his body into the brush and hightail it back to Smoke River to collect their blood money from Arbuckle. He prayed that a gunshot would be heard; if anyone *was* in the area, someone would know what happened to him and could tell Jess. *Jess. Oh, God, Jess.*

The trail ended abruptly at a vertical slab of vine-laced rock. Swarthy pulled his mount up, then turned it halfway around to intercept Cole.

He watched the stubby fingers reach for the revolver in his belt. *Dear God, take care of Jess. Don't let her see my body.*

He closed his eyes and waited.

Suddenly a sharp voice rang out from above him. "Drop the hardware! Hands in the air!"

"Wha—?" Swarthy's words choked off. Cole watched the sun-darkened man raise his thick arms over his head, followed by the other two.

The underbrush rustled and three men rose, rifles pointed down at the men who held him. Cole never thought he'd want to kiss a sheriff, but there was always a first time.

Sheriff Jericho Silver moved to jerk Swarthy off his horse and snap handcuffs on his wrists. Marshal Matt Johnson waved his rifle, and Jim and the third man sat without moving, hands raised high.

"Now," Jericho barked at the cowering fugitives, "dismount and put your hands behind you."

One of the men jabbed his boot heels into his horse, and instantly a rifle barked. Jim dismounted, cut his gaze to the side and went for his gun. Another rifle shot.

Matt Johnson cut the rope around Cole's wrists. "You okay, Cole?"

Cole gave a half laugh. "If you can convince me I'm not dreaming, or dead, then I'm okay."

"They're coming!" Noralee burst through the door of the *Sentinel* office. "The sheriff and two dead men, they're coming!" She danced up to Eli and tugged him by the hand out to the boardwalk.

Jessamine slowly lowered her pencil and laid it on her desk. Two dead men? *Oh, God.*

Was Cole one of them? She moved slowly to the doorway, slicked her perspiring palms against her green wool skirt and shaded her eyes against the winter sun.

Sheriff Silver was in the lead, followed by Wash Halliday and two horses with inert bodies slung across their backs. Last came Marshal Johnson and a third man.

The last man's garments were filthy with trail dust, his face bristly with whiskers and streaked with sweat. For a moment Jessamine thought it was a fourth outlaw, and then her breath hitched.

"Cole!" She dashed past Eli and Noralee and out into the street.

He reined up and sat looking down at her until she thought she would scream. Then he leaned half out of the saddle and closed his hands under her armpits. The next thing she knew she was being hauled sideways across his lap.

She buried her face against his shoulder and felt his body tremble. He pressed his face against her hair, tightened his arms around her and kneed the horse forward.

"Cole, thank God," she said when she could talk. "Thank God."

He held her without speaking until they reached the jail at the far end of town, and then he reined up.

He made no move to dislodge her or to dismount. Instead he brought his mouth to her ear.

"I need a bath and a shave, Jess." His breath was warm and rough against her cheek. "And then I need to take you to bed."

Marshal Johnson lifted her down and steadied her while Cole slowly dismounted. His motions were stiff, as if he hurt all over. Jess lifted one of his arms around her shoulders and slipped her free arm around his waist. Together they moved past a blubbering Noralee and a shiny-eyed Eli, who managed to reach out and pat Cole's free arm as they passed.

"Eli, get me some whiskey," Cole rasped. Then he dipped his head and pressed his bristly chin against Jess's hair. "Bath first."

An hour later he lurched through the door of her office and walked unsteadily up to her desk. "I'm not drunk, Jess. I just haven't slept much the past two days."

Without a word she rose and shut the door behind him. Then she marched to the window and turned the Closed sign to face the street.

Chapter Twenty

Upstairs in Jess's bedroom, Cole tumbled fully clothed onto the bed, and before she could skim off her skirt and shirtwaist, he was asleep.

He slept until past midnight while she held him, and when he woke he shed his shirt and jeans and stripped off her petticoat and the rest of her underthings and caught her trembling body under his.

He wanted to make it good for her, but he couldn't hold himself back. "Jess," he croaked. "Jess." He felt like weeping as he touched her and stroked her body. Her skin was warm and silky and smelled good. So good. He was hungry, desperate to be with her, inside her, and he guessed he was a little crazy.

But she said nothing, didn't stop him or urge him to take it slow, just rode with him, and when he was spent she held him close.

In the morning he looked down at her kiss-swollen lips and her dark lashes and wondered if he was dreaming. Or dead. No, not dead. He felt marvelously, miraculously alive after his night with Jess, and damn grateful. Made him think of all kinds of things, like how important Jess was to him and how short life could be. He didn't want to waste any more time without her.

All at once he realized what day it must be. Friday morning! And he had a newspaper to get out.

"Jess, wake up. I've got to—"

She opened her eyes and gave him a drowsy smile. "No, you don't, Cole. Eli and Noralee locked up the galleys last night. You can read your Friday edition at breakfast."

He stared at her. "You wrote the stories for my newspaper? All of them?"

"All except the editorial," she said. "I left that page blank."

An hour later, over platters of scrambled eggs and bacon, Cole avidly read every single typeset line of every single story Jess had written for him.

Lark Editor Disappears
Sheriff suspects foul play following election defeat of Conway Arbuckle.

He kept reading.

Conway Arbuckle Arrested!
Sentinel editor Jessamine Lassiter marches losing candidate to jail.

Cole clunked down his coffee cup. "Just how did
you do that?" he demanded.

Jessamine crunched into her fifth sourdough bis-
cuit slathered with strawberry jam. "With my new
derringer, of course."

Cole read on.

New Sheriff Recruited
Texas Ranger Anderson Rivera will assume
the Smoke River sheriff's position as Jericho
Silver takes new post as district judge.

He scanned the other headlines.

President Grant Opens New
East-West Railway

Sioux Nation on Warpath!
Indians Swear Vengeance
for Massacre

Music School Announces
Summer Operetta Plans

He read until Jess couldn't stand it another minute.

"Well? Is it all right?"

He scattered the pages onto the table. "It is very all right, Jess. In fact, it's so all right it's scary. You have a secret hankering to run two newspapers?"

She sent him an exasperated look. "Do I seem touched in the head? Ready to be locked up somewhere? How can you ask such a question?"

"Just checking. I wanted to make sure there was still room in this town for two newspapers."

"Two *competing* newspapers."

"Yeah," he said with a grin. "I guess we do have to compete. We need to keep up our circulation, and competition between the *Lark* and the *Sentinel* will do just that."

He reached across the table and took her hand. "Thanks, Jess. I owe you."

Jessamine broke her first story about the new sheriff in the Saturday edition of the *Sentinel*, devoting the lead article to the former Texas Ranger Anderson Rivera. Reading it over in his office that morning, Cole scratched his head.

Smoke River Welcomes
New Sheriff

Smoke River welcomes experienced tracker and lawman thirty-two-year-old Anderson Rivera. The new sheriff will be sworn in by Jericho Silver, the district judge, upon Rivera's arrival from Texas, which is expected within two weeks.

Colonel Rivera's father was well-known Texas rancher Don Luis Lopez-Rivera, originally of Chihuahua, Mexico.

His mother was the former Marguerite Anderson Cutty, of York, England. Both parents are deceased.

Jess's article went on to describe Rivera's education—eighth grade; military service—colonel in the Confederate army; and marital status—widowed.

When the *Lark* came out on Tuesday, Cole called Jess's opening bid and raised her ten.

New Sheriff a Mystery

New sheriff Anderson Rivera's arrival in Smoke River brings more questions than answers. First, who is this man? A Texas Ranger, we are told. Why, one wonders, does Smoke River need a Texas Ranger to keep the peace? Second, what's in it for him? The sheriff of a small Oregon town isn't nearly as well paid as a Texas Ranger.

So, I ask again: Who is this man?

The new sheriff will board with Ilsa Rowell, who is his half sister.

But that isn't the most interesting thing. What's most interesting is that our new sheriff's philosophy of peacekeeping is unusual, and it consists of merely two words: "Whatever works."

Contacted by telegraph in his native Dry Creek, Texas, Colonel Rivera expressed interest in his new territory in Oregon with the following, and I quote: "Are the women pretty?"

Finally this reporter uncovered one other intriguing item: our new sheriff sings bass.

"Sings bass!" Jessamine spluttered over a cup of tea at the restaurant. "Of what relevance is that?"

"Human interest," Cole said.

She glared across the table at him. "And 'Are the women pretty?' What's that got to do with law enforcement?"

She couldn't believe Cole had dug up more information about Rivera than she had. In the past three days she'd sent seven telegrams, and all the replies had been full of relevant information. But Cole had outsmarted her by reporting on personal items, which would surely titillate newspaper readers.

Why didn't I think of that?

"Excuse me," she said with frost in her voice, "I have another editorial to write." She rose, twitched her gray skirt into place and marched out.

She returned to the *Sentinel* office in high dudgeon. "Why didn't I think of that?" she complained to Eli.

"Ya did, Jess," the old man allowed. "Ya just weren't nosy enough. Besides, you didn't know about his half sister."

"Oh, I detest that man," she fumed.

Eli snickered. "Which man, Anderson Rivera or Cole Sanders?"

"Cole Sanders," she retorted.

"Nah," he drawled, "you don't detest Cole. You detest being outdone, that's what."

"Hush up, Eli. I most certainly have not been 'outdone.' We'll just see who's 'outdone.'"

Eli rolled his eyes and crunched into another one of his oatmeal cookies.

But Eli was right in one regard. Ever since his kidnapping, she and Cole were doing two contradictory things; on the one hand, each time their eyes met across a desk or a dining table or a courtroom, they looked at each other differently. And when she was anywhere near him she wanted to reach out and touch him, just to be sure he was really there.

On the other hand, she often found herself withdrawing from him, asking him to speak to her as a fellow journalist and not as a…well, lover. And Cole took pains to honor her request.

Absently she reached for the last of Eli's cookies.

Chapter Twenty-One

While the town breathlessly awaited the arrival of Anderson Rivera, their new sheriff, Cole decided to run a series of human interest articles on the man. On a sunny Monday morning, he went from the restaurant onto a tree-shaded side street and found Ilsa Rowell, Billy's mother, bent over a washtub in her backyard, scrubbing mud off a pair of the boy's jeans.

"Mrs. Rowell?"

"Yes?" She didn't straighten up. She didn't even look up, just kept drubbing the garment up and down on the corrugated tin washboard.

"I understand our new sheriff, Anderson Rivera, is a relative of yours," he ventured.

"Yes, he is. He's my brother. Actually he's my half brother. His ma married my pa and then she had me."

"I see. Was this in Oregon?"

"Texas. Down near the Rio Grande. My brother is—was—a Texas Ranger."

Cole already knew that from Jessamine's article in the *Sentinel*, but he wanted something more. Something intriguing. Something sensational, if he could pry it out of Ilsa.

"Why did he quit the Rangers?"

"Good question," she said shortly.

"What would you guess his reason was?"

Ilsa straightened and propped soapy hands on her hips. "I sure don't know, Mr. Sanders. I never did understand Sonny, and when I was growing up he made it pretty clear that nothing he did or said or even thought was any of my business."

"Sonny?"

"That's what his pa called him. I do, too." She bent again over the washboard.

"Did you like him? Was he a good brother?"

That brought her ramrod straight, a sopping pair of jeans in her hand. "A good brother? Mr. Sanders, I worshipped Sonny, I really did. I liked him, I really liked him. Still do, as a matter of fact. He's a good man, just…private."

Private, huh? Cole twiddled his pencil between his thumb and forefinger. He was getting nowhere with Ilsa Rowell. To all appearances, the new sheriff's past was dull as dishwater. Maybe the man was curled inward tighter than a corkscrew.

Or maybe, just maybe, the man had a secret of some kind, one that would warrant leaving the Texas Rangers and coming a thousand miles north to a tiny out-of-the-way place like Smoke River. A scandal, maybe? A killing? A woman?

Ilsa gathered up an armload of wet clothes. "Excuse me, Mr. Sanders." She sent him a look and then shouldered her way past him to the clothesline in the backyard.

Cole sighed. He hadn't gotten the story he'd hoped for this morning, but he wasn't about to give up. Sheriff Anderson would be here within a week; Cole would wait. And when the man came to town, he would sharpen up his pencils and pounce.

On the second Monday in January, Jess turned up at the meeting room behind the barbershop to cover Jericho Silver's swearing-in ceremony. She was an hour early.

Nearly a hundred townspeople had gathered to witness the event, but the closer the hour drew, the more curious she became. Why wasn't Cole present? Was he out covering a more interesting piece of news? The thought made her squirm.

What am I missing?

At two o'clock sharp, tall, tanned Jericho Silver in pressed jeans and a crisp white shirt took his place before Federal Marshal Matt Johnson, who was entrusted with the investiture proceedings on behalf of Governor Morse in Portland.

"Raise your right hand, Jericho," the marshal instructed. Maddie Silver stepped up to her husband's side and slipped a Bible under his left palm. While she swiped tears of pride off her cheeks, Jericho swore to uphold the laws of the state of Oregon and to be fair and impartial in dispensing justice.

It was thrilling to watch. Jess felt her own eyes tear up right along with Maddie's. Jericho Silver, the orphan boy from Portland of unknown parentage, a man who had pulled himself up by his bootstraps, who had built a reputation for toughness and even-handed justice, had beaten rich, puffed-up Conway Arbuckle fair and square at the polls. Oh, she did love democracy!

After the ceremony, Jess drew Maddie aside for an in-depth interview about finding herself the wife of the new district judge. But all the while she was scribbling on her notepad, she wondered where Cole was and what her competitor was doing. Was she missing something newsworthy?

If so, what on earth was it?

She wanted to ask Maddie something personal, something with the human interest aspect Cole was always yammering about, but she hesitated to voice it. Oh, well, why not? Cole said human interest was what sold newspapers.

"Maddie," she began, her tooth-nibbled pencil poised over her notepad, "what is it really like, being married to the sheriff and now the Lake County district judge?"

Maddie laughed. "I'm not married to either the

sheriff or the district judge. I am married, *very* married, to a man, Jericho Silver. And believe me, Jessamine, that is a challenge." The young woman's cheeks flushed a pretty rose color. "And," she added, her voice dropping, "a great pleasure, as well."

Well! She couldn't print that!

"I understand you have a career, too, Maddie, as a Pinkerton agent. How do you and Jericho carve out any time together? Especially now that you are the parents of twins?"

Maddie leaned toward her and lowered her voice still further. "At night, Jessamine. Jericho and I are together at night. All night."

"Heavens, I can't quote that, Maddie. It's too personal."

"Well, yes, I suppose it is," Maddie said with a laugh. "I thought you wanted to know, as a woman and not just as a newspaper editor."

"Yes," Jess said quickly. "I do."

"You know, Jessamine—and I don't want to be quoted on this—but I didn't really want to marry Jericho and settle down in Smoke River."

Jess stared at her. "You didn't? Why did you, then?"

Maddie sighed. "Why does any woman marry a man and settle down? I wanted to be with Jericho. And I wanted that more than I wanted anything else."

"Oh." Jess was not often at a loss for words, but at this moment "Oh" was all she could think of to say. *Maddie wanted to be with Jericho more than she wanted anything else.* How extraordinary.

After another half hour of talk so personal Jess knew she could never use it in a news story, she said goodbye, hugged Maddie and returned to the *Sentinel* office.

The afternoon dragged on and on and still Cole did not appear. She loaded her afternoon edition into Teddy MacAllister's saddlebags and helped Billy Rowell stuff his sack full, saw both boys off and then walked down to the restaurant for supper. Alone.

While she poked at her chicken croquettes and mashed potatoes, she thought about Jericho and Maddie Silver.

What *was* it like to be married? And have two careers?

When the latest edition of the *Lark* came out, Jess received another shock.

Sheriff Anderson Rivera
to Arrive in Smoke River
Tuesday Afternoon

Pooh! That was simply not possible. Texas was over a thousand miles from Oregon. Even if the man rode fifty miles a day, it would take him twenty days to get here. Cole was bluffing. He had to be. Besides, *today* was Tuesday.

She charged across the street and collided with Noralee at the front door of the *Lark* office.

"Didja see him, Miss Jessamine? Didja? Oh, he's so tall and…and…he takes great big steps!"

"Your imagination is working overtime, Noralee. Sheriff Rivera won't be here for at least two weeks."

"But he *is* here, honest. I saw him."

Jessamine followed the burbling girl into Cole's office.

"It's true, Jess," Cole said calmly from behind his desk. "Rivera's here."

"Impossible," she said.

Cole's dark eyebrows went up. "Why is it impossible?"

"Because a man, even a paragon of law enforcement, as Anderson Rivera is purported to be, cannot ride a thousand miles in—"

Cole laughed aloud. "Who says he rode?"

"Well, how did he get here if he—"

Cole stood up. Because he was towering over her, Jess had to look up at him. "Stop and think a minute, Miss Thinks-She-Knows-Everything."

Her face changed. "Oh, no," she breathed. "The railroad."

For a moment Cole almost felt sorry for her. Almost. "Yes, the railroad," he echoed.

"But…but what about his horse?"

"The man hasn't got just one horse, Jess. He's

got a whole remuda. He's hired someone to drive them north."

Noralee giggled over her type stick, and in that instant Cole realized he'd made a tactical error. He wanted to compete with Jess, not make her so mad she'd never let him get close enough to kiss her again.

He reached his hand out to touch her arm, but she jerked away with a sniff.

"Jess..."

"Oh, go to the devil, Cole." She pivoted and swept out so fast her skirt got caught when the door slammed.

"You don't understand girls, Mr. Sanders," Noralee said quietly.

What? He did, too, understand girls. He understood Jess well enough to take her to bed and make love to her, didn't he? What wasn't "understanding" about that?

But under his shirt collar he began to sweat. He couldn't ask Noralee about it, but he wondered...

At least he *thought* he knew about women. About Jess.

Didn't he?

Noralee sighed, and then sighed again. Cole glanced over to see the girl's hands lying idle on the typesetting table, her attention riveted on something outside the front window. He followed her gaze.

Anderson Rivera, the new sheriff, was tying up

his horse at the rail in front of the Golden Partridge Saloon.

"Noralee?"

No answer.

"Noralee, are you all right?"

She turned dazed brown eyes to him. "What?" She released another long breath of air. "No, I am not all right, Mr. Sanders. My brain is chattering inside my head. I can't think. I am… I am in love."

Cole glanced out the window again. The only thing he saw was the sheriff's bay mare, standing quietly at the hitching rail. "With a horse?" he inquired.

"Oh, no," she moaned. "With *him*. With the new sheriff."

Cole bit his tongue to keep from laughing. When he could speak he said, "He's a bit old for you, don't you think?"

"No," she whispered. "I'm gonna grow up real fast, and then he won't be too old at all."

Great jumping jennies! He racked his brain for the right thing to say to the girl. "Noralee, I'm sure you will be a lovely young woman when you are grown-up. No doubt in a few years you will have many suitors, and—"

"I don't want many suitors," she murmured. "I just want him."

Cole walked twice around his desk and stopped near the table where the girl sat, mesmerized into immobility. "Uh, Noralee, while you're growing up, do you think you could set some type for me?"

"What? Oh, sure, Mr. Sanders." She didn't move.

"Now?" he inquired in a gentle voice.

"What? Oh, sure, right away." Still she remained motionless on her stool.

"Right away *today*?" he pursued. Or would he have to wait until Sheriff Anderson Rivera emerged from the saloon, mounted his horse and moseyed on out of Noralee's view?

He exhaled a long breath. *Women.*

Chapter Twenty-Two

Cole decided he didn't like Anderson Rivera. Not because he was inefficient, or full of himself, which he wasn't. It was just…well, he couldn't exactly put his finger on what bothered him. The man partook of a friendly drink at the Golden Partridge of an evening, tipped his immaculate sand-colored Stetson to all the ladies, respectable or otherwise, and took time to speak to the youngsters around town. He even treated them to chocolate cookies at Uncle Charlie's Bakery.

The string of horseflesh that paraded down Main Street two weeks later were such fine-looking specimens, even after a journey of a thousand miles up through the Texas and Arizona desert, that men poured out of businesses and the saloon and lined the street to ogle them, especially the spirited Appaloosa that led the herd.

Deputy Sandy Boggs let his admiration for the

man be known in no uncertain terms, and Noralee
Ness went into such a trance whenever the new sheriff stepped into the *Lark* office that Cole had to prod
her back to setting type. The girl was so moony she
started making spelling errors, which she had *never*
done, even when working under a tight deadline.

Already Rivera had brought in the outlaw who
had robbed the Gillette Springs Bank, and he'd re-
covered all the money in the bargain. Billy Rowell,
Rivera's nephew, had started standing so straight
and proud Cole wondered if his momma was putting starch in his overalls.

It seemed that everybody in Smoke River loved
the man. Everyone except Cole. Not only that, but he
couldn't tell how Jessamine regarded the new sheriff. He watched her bustle about town, her notepad
clutched in one hand and a fistful of pencils in the
other, reporting on the wheat crop; the baby shower
for Ellie Johnson, the marshal's wife; the new violin
teacher the music school had hired; even the sale of
Miss Lucy's place over on Maple Street. Cole would
sure like to know just how Jess had managed to un-
cover *that* piece of information.

She also reported on how plans for the summer
operetta, *Lady Marmalade's Suitors*, were shaping
up. Casting for the principal singers would start in
April. Music would be provided by Ike Bruhn on guitar and mandolin and Anderson Rivera on his fiddle.
Hot damn, the man could play the fiddle?

Dressmaker Verena Forester would design and sew costumes for the dancing girls. *Dancing girls!* Cole figured Sheriff Rivera would be needed more to keep order among the males during any performance with dancing girls than to play his fiddle.

Jess was always busy these days. Cole had to admit she was doing a fine job of competing with the *Lark*; she matched him scoop for scoop, often publishing stories he'd thought he had an exclusive on. But he managed to return the favor so often that whenever they shared breakfast or a late-afternoon cup of coffee, she took to clapping her hands over her notepad so he couldn't read what she was writing.

She still smiled at him with those huge gray-green eyes that made his heart skip three beats. And she still worried her lower lip between her teeth, which left him hard and hot and hungry for a lot more than scrambled eggs and bacon.

This morning Cole looked up to see Sheriff Rivera stride past the front window of the restaurant and Cole found himself watching Jess closely.

Her gaze flicked up, then focused on the man's long legs.

"Noralee's right," she murmured. "He does take giant steps."

Cole stared at her. "What's that got to do with the price of corn?"

She worried her lower lip. "Why, nothing at all."

He snaked a hand across the table and grasped her wrist. "Dammit, Jess, don't do that!"

She dimpled and he almost choked on his coffee. Hell's bells, when had she developed a dimple? He thought he'd seen every kind of smile that ever crossed her face; how could he have missed that dimple? He wanted to run his tongue into that sweet little curved indentation in her cheek.

"Cole, whatever is the matter? You look very odd."

He released her wrist and sucked in his breath. "I told you what getting your lips all rosy like that does to me."

She nodded, then stared past him out the window. Oh, hell, she wasn't even listening to him.

She gave her lower lip another nibble and he clenched his jaw. She was driving him crazy.

"Hell's bells, Jess, you want me to kiss you right here in the restaurant in front of everybody?"

"Oh. I forgot."

He stared at her. "You forgot?" She *forgot*?

Dimples again. His shirt collar constricted his Adam's apple. He undid the top button.

"Cole?"

He swallowed. "Yeah?"

"Do you still want to?"

"Want to what?"

"Kiss me."

With a groan he bolted out of his chair, gripped

her shoulders and dragged her up to face him. "Yeah, I still want to." He covered her mouth and kissed her until his breath stopped.

It wasn't until he released her that he realized the restaurant was empty and Rita was busy in the kitchen. Thank God for that. He didn't want to play fast and loose with Jess's reputation. She wasn't the kind of girl a man dallied with just for the hell of it.

But God knew losing his wife was as close to hell as he ever wanted to get. He didn't dare risk being married to a woman ever again.

"God, Jess, don't tease me. I haven't kissed you in exactly six weeks and three days."

"You've been counting?"

"Damn right I've been counting."

"Good. I was beginning to wonder."

"What the—?" He groaned.

Jessamine thought his eyes couldn't get any narrower, but she was mistaken.

"Don't play games with me, Jess. You know I like kissing you. I'm trying to keep it under control."

She watched the struggle in his face. The pain in his eyes sent a shard of unease into her chest. "I don't mean to tease you, Cole. Or play games."

He just looked at her. "You know how hard it is for me to keep my hands off you?"

She swallowed.

"Listen, Jess, you know that losing my wife was… I can't do it again."

"What are you saying, Cole?"

"I'm saying…" He swallowed again. "I'm saying I can't bring myself to risk being married to a woman. Ever."

"Yes, of course, I understand that. It's something you've mentioned before. But there's something you don't know about me, Cole."

"Yeah? What's that?"

"I do not want to marry anyone. I will never marry. I care about you, Cole, but I am not looking for marriage."

He looked as if a horse had just kicked him. "Care to tell me why?"

"It's a legal thing. In Oregon the minute a man and a woman get married, the woman loses control over her property. It falls to her husband. The truth is, I don't want to lose my family newspaper to anyone. Not even you."

Again, he just looked at her, a muscle twitching in his jaw, his fists clenched at his sides. "That's what the law says, is it?"

"Yes, it is. I checked in Jericho Silver's law books and—"

"You think you might lose control over your newspaper, is that it?"

"Exactly. So you can relax, Cole. And…" She laid her fingers against his stubbly cheek. "…that means you can kiss me whenever you want."

He caught her wrist. "Not so fast. You sure about what the law says?"

"About a married woman's property? Yes, I'm sure. That's why—"

"I heard you the first time," he growled.

She gazed up into his troubled blue eyes and wondered why she felt as if she'd laced up her corset way too tight. She didn't like the constricted feeling inside her chest, or the funny hot burning in her throat or the hungry ache that was blooming below her belly.

What she wanted was for Cole Sanders to kiss her. A lot.

She also knew she couldn't have it both ways. Since neither of them wanted a permanent relationship, she could either love him and be with him or avoid tempting him. To be fair, she couldn't continue to torture him; he deserved better.

She expelled a long sigh and fought down an overwhelming urge to cry. Mercy, she hadn't felt this bereft since her brother, Miles, was killed.

"Miss Jessamine?"

Jess pivoted to see Noralee Ness timidly edging through the front door of the *Sentinel* office. "Yes, Noralee? What is it?"

The girl glanced at Eli, bent over his font case, and tipped her head toward the far corner. "Can I speak to you in private?" she whispered.

Jess followed Noralee to the niche by the doorway.

"Miss Jessamine, how does a girl get beautiful?"

Jess blinked. "Beautiful? You mean a pretty dress and curls?"

"No, I mean beautiful all over. Like you."

"Honey, I'm not beautiful all over. I wear proper clothes and wash my hair twice a week, but that's all."

"You smell good, and your cheeks are pink," Noralee said softly. "And your eyebrows look like, um, like upside-down smiles."

Jess blinked again. "Upside-down smiles? What an original description. I do believe you have a talent for words, Noralee."

The girl sighed. "You really think so? Do you think I could write a…a love letter?"

"Well, you *could*, I'm sure. But whether you *should* is another matter entirely. Besides, I'm not sure a love letter is the way to a boy's heart. Can you bake cookies?"

"Cookies! He wouldn't want any old cookies!"

"I wouldn't be too sure about that, Noralee. Most males are very partial to cookies."

Noralee brightened. "And while I made cookies I could be growing beautiful, couldn't I, Miss Jessamine? Oh, thank you! I knew you'd know what to do."

She was out the door before Jess could open her mouth. She stood looking after her, skipping across the street to the *Lark* office. What strange notions girls got when someone plucked at their heartstrings. Women, too, she acknowledged.

Eli's dry voice made her jump. "It's hell to be young, ain't it?"

She spoke without thinking. "Sometimes it's hell to be twenty-two."

"Yep. I figured that. Got you all tied up in an eight-way knot, huh?"

"Nonsense! I am not tied up at all. I am as care-free as a song sparrow."

Eli didn't respond, and Jess sent up a little prayer begging forgiveness for her lie.

An obviously pregnant Ellie Johnson stopped in at the restaurant and made a beeline for the table in the corner where Cole and Jessamine sat over breakfast. "I'm so pleased to find you two together," Ellie said.

"Mrs. Johnson." Cole instantly rose and surrendered his chair, then snagged another from an adjacent table.

"Thank you, Cole." Ellie sank onto the padded seat and turned a beaming smile on him and then Jess. "I need you both."

"What for?" Jessamine blurted.

"Jessamine means," Cole inserted dryly, "what can we do for you?"

Ellie grinned. "You may recall that we are planning to stage an operetta this summer? *Lady Marmalade's Suitors*?"

"Of course," Jess said. "I was going to run a story about it in the *Sentinel*. Have you chosen the cast?"

Rita appeared, a coffeepot in one hand and a china teapot in the other. "Miz Johnson, would you like coffee? Tea?"

"Coffee, please, Rita. I need to stay on my toes today."

She turned to Jessamine. "No," she said, "I haven't chosen the cast yet. I'm holding tryouts tomorrow and—"

"You'd like us to announce it in our newspapers," Cole supplied.

"Well, that, too," Ellie responded with a grin. She accepted a full mug of coffee and dumped in cream until it threatened to overflow.

Jess frowned. "Too? What does that mean?"

"Um, well…" Ellie sent a questioning look at Cole. "I would like you to try out for a part."

"Oh, no," Cole protested instantly. "I don't sing in public. I told you that when I tried out for the choir, remember?"

"Yes, you do," Jess contradicted. "You sang in the *Messiah* at Christmas, remember?"

Oh, Lord yes, he remembered. He remembered the thrill of standing close enough to Jess to brush her arm, hearing her voice blend with his and later kissing her until his brain softened into molasses and making love to her as if there would never be a tomorrow.

"Yeah, I remember. But singing with a choir isn't like standing up on a stage, alone, and singing in front of a real audience. Alone," he repeated.

"There are three parts for male singers," Ellie said.

"You could do that, Cole," Jess said with an encouraging smile.

"And," Ellie went on, "there are two female lead roles. Jessamine?" She sent Jess an expectant look.

"Oh, no, I—I am really busy at the *Sentinel* with, um, the Fourth of July celebration. Oh, and the Ladies' Hat Competition and—"

"Ladies' Hat Competition?" Cole interrupted. "What the heck is that?"

"You wouldn't be interested," Jess said in a patient voice. "It's a ladies' matter."

"Maybe not, but my newspaper would be interested. News is news, remember?"

"Stop it, you two," Ellie interrupted. "Humor me. I would very much like your help in two ways. First, to announce tryouts in your newspaper, and second, I would like both of you to show up and—" she paused and looked from Cole to Jessamine "—try out."

Half the population of Smoke River showed up at the music hall for the operetta tryouts. Uncle Charlie brought three overflowing trays of oatmeal and cinnamon cookies, and when director Ellie Johnson suggested that the rotund Chinese man audition for the part of Ricardo the Magician, Charlie bowed low.

"No sing," he said. "But make good magic, like in China."

"Oh?" Ellie studied the grinning man with heightened interest. "Could you come back later and give me a demonstration?"

"Ah, no, Missus." Charlie waved his hands over young Teddy MacAllister's head and pulled a shiny quarter from behind one ear and a perfect yellow rosebud from the other.

"Hey, how'd you do that?" Teddy demanded.

"Magician never tell how," Charlie said with an enigmatic smile. "But you wash front window tomorrow, and I show you more."

"You're hired!" Ellie exulted. "I don't care if you can't sing a single note, Charlie, you are a real magician!"

"Oh, can sing, too," the Chinese man corrected. "Just not want to."

Cole Sanders, seated behind Ellie, laughed out loud. The director swiveled her head and pointed a long finger at him. "You're next, Cole."

"Aw, now, Ellie…" Beside him, Jessamine smiled broadly.

"Sing," Ellie commanded. "Anything but 'Clementine.'"

Cole swallowed hard and opened his lips. "'I knew she was the one when she loaded up her gun and—'"

"That's enough, Cole. You're perfect for the part of Sir Sandwich."

Jessamine was still giggling when Ellie pointed at her. "Miss Lassiter? Sing something, please."

Jess blinked. It wasn't an invitation; it was an order. "Uh, well, let me see. How's this?" She drew in a breath.

"'She peered hard down the barrel and watched his blue eyes narrow, then—'"

"Hired!" Ellie chortled. "Jessamine, you will make an admirable Lady Marmalade." She had to raise her voice over Cole's laughter.

"I don't know about you two," the music director muttered under her breath. "Positively…well, shame-lessly…shameless."

Alto Ardith Buchanan won the part of Lady Marmalade's lady-in-waiting, and Cole, Ike Bruhn and Anderson Rivera were cast as the three suitors. The sheriff would play his fiddle.

Cole groaned under his breath. *Anderson Rivera.* He sure hoped none of the suitors got to kiss Lady Marmalade. Especially not Sheriff Rivera.

Noralee Ness won the part of Miss Evangeline, and Billy Rowell ended up as Picklerelish.

At the end of the evening, Cole offered to walk Jessamine home, but he had to practically arm-wrestle her away from Anderson Rivera, who was standing next to her—way too close—demonstrating a sudden interest in Jess's gift for improvising verse.

Cole didn't realize his fists were clenched until he tried to stuff his hands into his trouser pockets.

Chapter Twenty-Three

Rita plopped her coffeepot down on the table and scowled at the two diners facing each other across an expanse of white linen tablecloth. Land sakes, they weren't even looking at each other, much less talking! Each newspaper editor had his—or her—head hidden behind the pages of the other's morning edition. Not only that, but neither Cole Sanders nor Jessamine Lassiter looked up, even when she refilled their cups. For the third time.

Only when she retreated to the kitchen did she hear a single word spoken.

"Kinda pointed," Cole said.

Jessamine raised her coffee cup to her lips without glancing up. "No more so than *your* editorial."

"Yeah, but my editorial is more accurate.

She stifled a grin. "Prove it." She loved bantering with Cole. He made her squirm, and she made him laugh.

"Jess, your editorial is downright opinionated."

"An editorial doesn't have to be accurate," she challenged. "An editorial is just that, an opinion. And in *this* case, *my* opinion on the matter is better than *yours*."

Cole snorted. "But at least the editor's opinion has to be based on facts."

"Does not."

He hid his smile behind the newspaper he held before his face. "Another thing, Jess. Writing-wise, you're stuck in another alphabetical rut. This time it's *J* words. *Jaundiced. Jounced. Jerry-rigged.*"

"I like *J* words," she quipped. *"Jumpy...joyful... jittery,"* she recited. "So there. And may I point out that you're awfully fond of *M* words this week? *Murderous. Manacled. Mayhem.*"

"And I believe," he said dryly, "that it's *juryrigged*, not *jerry-rigged*."

"It is? Are you sure?"

"I'm sure. Kinda expected you to know the difference."

"There's a difference? I thought it was just a matter of spelling."

"Or misspelling," he said blandly.

She leaned across the table toward him. "Oh, Cole, I do like it when we discuss things. It's...stimulating."

He barked out a laugh. "Stimulating? 'Stimulating' would be reading an editorial of yours without a lot of hyperbole."

"Ah, yes, hyperbole," she mused aloud. She peeked out from behind the propped-up page of the *Lark*. "That's when someone tries to make his readers forget the facts, isn't it?"

"Hyperbole," he muttered, lowering his newspaper so their eyes met, "is what a woman does every time she smears rouge all over her cheeks."

She gave a delighted chirp of laughter. "My, that *is* clever. Personally I have never worn rouge. Papa said it wasn't proper."

"You don't need rouge, Jess," he said with a smile. "You're blushing."

"Oh." She bit her lip and Cole sucked in a breath.

"Let's get back to *manacled* and *mayhem*, shall we?" she said. "Those are perfectly good words for that snake Conway Arbuckle."

"He'll go to prison, Jess. I figure we're just helping him along. It won't be *jury-rigged* when he comes to trial."

She laughed. He'd never heard a woman's laugh he liked better than Jess's. Half the fun of their twice-weekly newspaper postmortems across the restaurant dining table was exchanging barbs with her.

Out of the corner of his eye, he saw Rita watching them, a puzzled look on her shiny face. He felt halfway sorry for the waitress. Weeks went by when he and Jess bantered back and forth across platters of eggs and bacon and biscuits. He guessed Rita couldn't figure out if they were friends or enemies.

Now that he thought about it, maybe that was a valid question. Lately he didn't know himself. Jess could be pointed, amusing, determined and playful, all at one sitting. It was damn hard to keep up with her, but it sure kept him on his toes.

As long as she doesn't nibble on her bottom lip.

He darted a look at her, then purposefully looked away. "Are you covering the dance out at Jensen's barn on Saturday?" he asked.

She blinked. "'Covering'? You mean gathering news?"

"Yeah."

"I rather thought a dance was an opportunity for a person to dance," she said tartly.

"That, too," he acknowledged. "Also good for finding out the latest news and gossip. I understand that Sheriff Walks-on-Water Rivera will be there."

Her dark eyebrows rose. "Walks on water?"

"Noralee is so swoony over Anderson Rivera you'd think he'd climbed down from Mount Olympus just to be the sheriff of Smoke River."

"You mean Valhalla, don't you? Mr. Rivera looks more Viking than Greek to me."

Cole groaned under his breath. Viking, Greek. It was bad enough that his typesetter was all aflutter over the man; an all too visceral part of him didn't want Jess to be smitten, as well.

Hell's bells, she was biting her lip again. He pushed away from the table and stood up.

"Where are you going?" she asked. "We aren't finished with our postmortem yet."

"I'm finished," Cole said in a tight voice. "I'll rent a buggy and drive you out to Jensen's on Saturday night if you'd like."

"Yes, thank you, Cole. On the way back to town we can compare notes on all the news and gossip. I look forward to it."

Cole folded his copy of the *Sentinel* under his arm and studied her rosy upturned face. He could hardly wait. But what he looked forward to wasn't talking with Jess; it was dancing with her.

Music floated on the evening air as Cole maneuvered the buggy close to Peter and Roberta Jensen's handsome red barn. He parked the rig among the horses and buckboards gathered in front of the structure, handed Jess down and took her elbow.

She looked so beautiful tonight he could scarcely breathe. Her dark blue skirt hugged the curve of her hips and swirled gracefully about her black button-up shoes. The lacy pink shirtwaist swelled in all the right places. He swallowed and looked off across a just-plowed field.

The minute Jess was inside she unwrapped the knit blue shawl about her shoulders, drew a notepad and a pencil from her skirt pocket and headed for the chairs lining the plank dance floor where a row of onlookers sat chatting. Cole watched her make a beeline for Jericho and Maddie Silver, rocking their twin babies in two matching wicker laundry baskets.

Well, shoot. He wanted Jess dancing in his arms, not taking notes for her newspaper. He concentrated on the fiddle and guitar music and let his attention drift until it landed on the new sheriff, Anderson Rivera. His tall, spare frame moved purposefully toward the bar made of pine two-by-twelves balanced between two stacked apple crates. Cole watched the man speak at length to the bartender, Seth Ruben, down a cup of lemonade—*lemonade?*—and stride back to the dance floor.

Cole stepped up to the bar. "Seth," he greeted the paunchy man uncorking a fifth of whiskey.

"Cole. New sheriff sure don't drink much."

"Oh, yeah?"

"Been here two hours, and all he's had is lemonade."

"Clean and sober man, maybe. Pour me a shot."

Seth snorted. "Nah. More'n likely he doesn't want liquor on his breath for the ladies. Jest watch him." The bartender jerked his chin toward the dance floor.

Rivera was dancing with the widowed Elvira Sorensen. When the two-step concluded, the sheriff escorted the tall, gaunt woman back to her chair and then whirled pudgy Roberta Jensen out onto the floor. Then it was Zinnia Langfelter, the undertaker's daughter, and then old Mrs. Hinksley, the retired schoolteacher from Ohio who was eighty if she was a day. The elderly lady's snow-white head bobbed in time to the music while Rivera spun her around and around in a waltz. Next he engaged Maddie Silver in a spirited two-step.

After Maddie, Rivera bent over the hand of Ardith Buchanan, politely asking her to dance. Cole groaned. Noralee would be so jealous and distracted he might as well kiss Monday's galley proofs goodbye.

Suddenly he understood what the man was doing. The new sheriff was methodically working his way around the room, dancing once with every female at the gathering. Cole watched his progress and scratched his head. What did he think he was doing, running for office? Great jumping jennies, he already *had* the office.

Rivera's next target was Jessamine Lassiter. *Oh, no, you don't, you bastard. Keep your hands off my—* His what? His reaction brought him up short with a sucker punch to the gut. Jess didn't belong to him. She owed him nothing. Other than groin-tightening kisses and way too few nights of unforgettable lovemaking, he had no claim on her.

Jess didn't belong to him. He had no claim on her because…*because, you damn fool, you've never claimed her!*

All at once he found himself asking a surprisingly painful question: What exactly did Jessamine Lassiter mean to him?

The question made his head spin. Maybe he'd step over to the bar again for another stiff whiskey and think this whole mess over.

"Back so soon?" Seth asked with a knowing grin.

"Yeah. Make it a double this time."

"Got woman trouble?"

"How'd you guess?" Cole growled.

"Aw, it ain't hard," Seth said in a sympathetic drawl. "The minute you fancy a woman, you got trouble."

Cole saluted the man with his glass, downed the contents in one gulp and turned back to the dance floor. Gritting his teeth, he searched for Jess, and when he found her in Rivera's arms he reached behind him and shoved his shot glass back toward Seth.

With a chuckle the bartender splashed in another two fingers of whiskey and slid it back within Cole's reach.

Cole didn't notice. His attention was riveted on Jess and Rivera. He could see her lips moving, making conversation or maybe asking questions, and he tightened his jaw until his teeth hurt.

Admit it, you selfish bastard. You don't want Jess to like him.

He watched her gaze up into the tall sheriff's face and folded his hands into fists. He knew just how she looked, her green eyes wide-open and eager, her mouth soft and sweet and…

God, please don't let her nibble her lips! The man was only human.

He gripped his whiskey, took a deep breath and tossed back every drop.

Noralee Ness smoothed the lace on the sleeves of her best blue gingham dress and said a prayer. *Please, please, Lord, let Sheriff Rivera ask me to dance. Please.*

She watched him across the expanse of plank flooring and wondered why the arms of the banjo and fiddle player were moving but making no noise. The low buzzing inside her head shut out everything in the Jensens' cavernous barn except the thudding of her heart.

If *he* asked her to dance, she vowed she wouldn't miss a step, music or no music. Whatever it was, a waltz, a schottische, a slow two-step or a fast polka, she would keep up with him; she just knew she would.

He looked so tall and handsome it made her throat ache. She couldn't keep her eyes off him, couldn't look anywhere else except at his long legs and broad shoulders, and she followed his every move with glazed eyes.

Now he was dancing with Maddie Silver. When he returned Maddie to her seat beside her husband, the sheriff bowed over the hand of Ardith Buchanan, the schoolmarm, seated next to Maddie. He swung the white-haired lady out onto the floor in a waltz that made her head bob and swoop in time to some music Noralee still could not hear.

Next it was the widow Sorensen again and then… Suddenly Noralee sucked in her breath. Sheriff Rivera was methodically working his way around the room, moving from one woman to the one sitting next to her, dancing with each one in turn.

Her heart skittered wildly. All she had to do was be the next female person in the seated row of onlookers and Sheriff Rivera would eventually invite *her* onto the floor.

It would all be so simple! She sped over to the sidelines and planted herself next to the chair just vacated by Mrs. Sorensen. *I'm next! I'm next!*

The sheriff whirled past and Noralee devoured him with her eyes. How elegantly he danced! His feet never got tangled up in a woman's long skirt no matter how many flounces at the hem. And he didn't waste time talking, either.

That was just as well, since she knew she would be completely tongue-tied just looking at him up close. Had she remembered to dab some of Mama's toilet water behind her ears? Men liked that; Miss Jessamine said they did. And rouge…but she couldn't find any rouge in her mother's top bureau drawer. Surreptitiously she pinched her cheeks to make them rosy.

What about her breath? Did it smell of corn on the cob?

Or, God forbid, of the green onions she'd had at supper? She cupped her hand over her mouth and puffed out a breath, then quickly inhaled. No onion smell, just a hint of tomatoes. Oh, why, *why* had she not brushed her teeth before coming to the dance?

The polka with Mrs. Sorensen was ending. Noralee watched the sheriff escort her back to her seat and tried to stop herself from bouncing up and down in anticipation.

He was coming! He was coming right toward her!

She tried to smile in a ladylike way, demure but friendly. But Sheriff Rivera passed by her chair and asked Rachel Bluett to partner him. Rachel Bluett! Why, *she* could dance better than a red-haired stick like Rachel Bluett! Lots better.

Instantly she jolted to her feet and repositioned herself four seats down, next to a line of as yet undanced-with ladies. Only after she sank onto the bench did she realize the woman next to her was her mother. And her twin sister, Edith.

She moved over three places.

But when the music started up again, it was Edith who walked out with the sheriff. Her own sister! How *could* she?

Oh, the cruelty of it. She couldn't bear to watch. Her heart was cracking in two right down the middle.

"Noralee?"

Billy Rowell stood in front of her. "Wanna dance?"

Well, yes, she wanted to dance, but not with Billy Rowell. Would it be impolite to refuse him and then step out onto the floor with Sheriff Rivera?

She moaned under her breath. Yes, it would be. "Um, well, I…uh…"

Just then the music stopped. The sheriff brought Edith back to her seat and asked the next woman, Ivy Bruhn, wife of the sawmill owner, to dance. The fiddle struck up another waltz.

"Yes," she blurted. "I'll dance with you, Billy." At least if she was out on the floor she would be that much closer to the sheriff. She could watch his face, maybe even hear what he was saying to his partner.

Billy Rowell danced like a wooden soldier. They circled twice around the floor and all at once he halted. "Noralee, stop leading."

"Oh. Sorry," she mumbled.

"S'okay. I don't dance too good anyway."

Out of the corner of her eye, she saw Sheriff Rivera return Lucy to her seat and head for the bar at the far end of the room. Surely he didn't drink spirits?

No. It was a glass of lemonade he held to his lips. Lemonade! She made the best lemonade in town; everybody said so, even Edith. Maybe someday the sheriff would…or she could take a quart jar of her fresh-squeezed lemonade with just a tad extra sugar over to the sheriff's office.

Billy returned her to the bench on the sidelines, bowed politely—*bowed*? Billy *bowed*? Just like the sheriff?—and left her. As soon as his back was turned, Noralee scooted over two more places to her right and waited expectantly for Sheriff Rivera to appear before her.

Chapter Twenty-Four

Jessamine lifted her head, waiting for the sheriff to respond to her query. She'd asked him, politely, how he liked Smoke River so far.

"Fine," he said.

She waited. Was that all, just "fine"?

"Is there something in particular you find pleasing?" she inquired.

"Nope."

"Nothing? Are you used to towns as small as Smoke River?"

"Yep."

Jess bit her lip. "Well, what was your home in Texas like?"

"Small."

"How small? Did you have a church? Or a school-house?"

"Yep. Both."

"And?" She smiled up at him and held her breath.

"And what?"

Oh, for mercy's sake! "What was your town in Texas *like*?" She hoped her exasperation didn't show.

"Like…Texas."

Jess frowned. "Are you worried because I'm a newspaper editor? Is that why you are so, well, short-spoken?"

"Nope."

"Perhaps you are afraid I will misquote you?"

"Nope."

"Mr. Rivera, don't you *want* to talk to me?"

"Oh, sure. I'm talkin'."

No, you are not, she fumed. Or…a thought struck her. Maybe the man thought he *was* talking to her. Maybe he simply didn't have that much to say.

He might be tall and attractive, but as for *interesting*—that he most certainly was not. Perhaps if she were twelve years old, like Noralee, but she wasn't twelve. She was twenty-two years old, and she had a brain in addition to a pair of eyes, and she was bored by this man. *Bored.*

Suddenly it struck her as funny. She gulped back a giggle just as a warm hand slid about her waist and someone swung her out of Anderson Rivera's long arms. She swirled away into the arms of Cole Sanders. Her heart lifted.

"Oh, Cole, talk to me!"

"Wh-what?"

"Say something. Anything! I'm starved for conversation."

Cole looked down at her eager face. "I thought you *were* conversing. Looked like it anyway."

She hesitated. "You want the truth?"

"Yeah, tell me."

"The past fifteen minutes with Sheriff Rivera have been the dullest fifteen minutes I've ever spent."

"Is that right?" Cole worked to keep from grinning.

"Oh, yes, most definitely. Cole, it's no fun at all talking to a man with no observations or opinions or wit or…"

"Does he smell good?"

A laugh spluttered out of her mouth and she clapped her hand over her lips. "*Smell* good?"

"You know, like bay rum or tobacco smoke or peppermint?"

"Who cares how he smells? He doesn't *talk*!"

Cole pulled her close and hid his smile against her hair. "You like talking, huh?"

He felt her head dip in a nod. "I do. You know I do. I never realized how much until tonight. I love it when we talk, Cole. When you tease me and we argue and… Oh, Cole, you are so *not* like Sheriff Anderson Rivera!"

"Yeah?"

"You are smart. And well-educated. And witty. And…well, fun."

"Fun," he said uncertainly.

"Of course." She squeezed the hand that held hers. "I couldn't live without at least a little bit of laughter. Life is too short not to enjoy things. Not to laugh about things. There are enough sad and serious things in the world."

His heart flipped up into his throat and for a moment he couldn't speak.

"You do understand, don't you, Cole?"

Oh, God yes, he understood. He folded her hand in against his chest and tightened his arm around her. "You know I understand, Jess. And dammit to hell, you know—" he steadied his voice "—that I love you."

"Cole," she murmured.

"Yeah?"

"Kiss me."

"Right here? In front of Sheriff Rivera and everybody?"

"Yes," she breathed. "Right this instant. Especially in front of Sheriff Rivera and everybody."

"No," he whispered. "Come outside with me. I want to do this properly."

Cole walked her around the corner of the barn, turned her to face him and drew her soft body against his. His thoughts careened around in his brain like caged squirrels. When she tipped her face up, he settled his mouth over hers and let himself enjoy what she offered.

After a long interval, he heard her moan and he lifted his head slightly. His groin ached with the driving hunger inside him.

"What brought this on all of a sudden?" he said against her lips.

"Dancing with Anderson Rivera."

"How come you don't want *him* kissing you?"

"I should think that would be perfectly obvious," she murmured.

He kissed her again. "Tell me."

"I like you," she breathed. "I think I may even love you. And I hardly know Sheriff Rivera."

"That," he said dryly, "is one helluva comfort. What about when you *do* know Rivera better?"

Her warm breath gusted near his ear. "Then I'll want to kiss you some more."

All at once he had to set her apart from him. "Whoa, Jess. Slow down a minute."

She just looked at him, her eyes beginning to darken the way they had when they made love that first night. Mercy, that was way last Christmas. Oh, God. She had no idea how many nights since then he'd lain awake, aching for her. Damn long nights.

He unhooked her arms from around his neck. "Jess, right now I can back off, but if we keep this up much longer, I won't be able to."

"I don't want you to back off, Cole."

He let out a long breath. "Hell's bells, honey, I

thought you didn't want us to get serious. You're afraid of losing your newspaper, remember?"

"I do remember," she said quietly. "And I know you don't want a committed relationship, either." She stretched up on tiptoe and pressed her lips to his neck.

"Jess, dammit, stop kissing me," he groaned. "I want you like I've never wanted another woman, not even Maryann, but I'm only human."

"What do you want, Cole? Tell me?"

"Ought to be pretty obvious. I want to get in that buggy and drive back to town and take you to bed. I want to make love to you."

She gave him a long, misty-eyed look. "I'll get my shawl."

Upstairs in her room, Cole puffed out the candle on the nightstand and reached for her. "Seems like years since I've been close enough to you to—" he slipped free the top button of her silky pink shirtwaist "—take off your clothes."

He undid the rest of the buttons, slid the garment off her bare shoulder and pressed his lips against her warm skin. She tugged at his belt buckle.

Her fingers fluttered too close to his erection, and if she brushed against him he didn't think he could stand it. Quickly he stripped down to his underdrawers, then laid his hands at the fastening of her skirt.

She stepped out of the garment, and he carefully

worked the hairpins out of the low bun at the back of her neck and dropped them to the floor. Then he untied her petticoat and next the ribbon of her chemise. Finally he unhooked her corset, tossed it away and spread his hand over her breast.

She murmured something. He bent, pressed his face between her breasts and ran his tongue over one nipple. God, she was sweet.

She made another little sound, and he turned to her other nipple. She brought his hands to her waist, and he freed the button of her pantalets. They slithered over her hips, and he shrugged off his drawers and fell backward onto the bed, bringing her down with him.

Her hair spilled over her shoulders, and he gathered it up in his fist, then brought it to his nose. "You smell like ripe strawberries," he murmured.

"You smell like pine trees," she said. She surprised him by running her tongue down his neck to his breastbone, and then on to his nipple, lightly nipping it with her teeth. It felt so exquisite he wanted to weep.

"And," she breathed, "you taste like…late-summer plums."

He touched his hand to the back of her head to keep her mouth where it was, but she moved to his navel and then—*damn!*—she wrapped her fingers around his erect member and touched the tip with her tongue.

His breath hissed in. In the next instant she drew his hand away from her breast, then pushed it farther down. When he slid a finger into her velvety folds, she cried out, and the next thing he knew he was inside her, moving in rhythm with her breathing and praying he could last until her release.

He had made love with her only twice before; each time it had been different, once sweet and once desperate. Tonight it was both. He didn't know how it happened, but something with dark wings settled over him and bore him up and up until he couldn't breathe. He wanted to shout, but he couldn't make a sound, could only move inside her slick warmth and soar far, far away.

She made a sound and suddenly went still. He felt her sheath close tight around him and begin to pulse in warm waves, and that pushed him over the edge.

"Jess. *Jess.*"

It had never been like this before, with anyone.

It scared the hell out of him.

Her cheeks were wet with tears. He kissed her face, her neck, licked up the moisture with his tongue and heard her long drawn-out sigh.

"Oh, my," she said, a lazy smile in her voice.

"Jess." He did his best not to withdraw; he wanted to keep holding her close. "Jess, I don't believe what just happened."

"I do. It was beautiful, Cole. It is beautiful being with you. It always is."

But then her breathing hitched.

Cole ran his hand slowly down her arm. "What's wrong?"

"I am wondering whether I am being fair to you."

"To me? What about you? Your reputation could suffer. There could even be a child."

"My reputation won't suffer if we are discreet," she said. "And, if we are careful, there won't be a child."

"How do you figure that?"

"I talked to Maddie Silver about how she…well, her twins were conceived by accident, but before she even knew she was expecting, she and Jericho were married. Doc Dougherty told her there are safe days and unsafe days for women."

"So?"

"These are my 'safe' days."

"No," he said flatly. "I'm not going to gamble."

"But…but, Cole…"

He rolled to one side, taking her with him. "Let's get married."

"What?"

"I said—"

"I heard you. I just don't believe…how much whiskey have you drunk tonight?"

"Not enough, apparently. I'm stone-cold sober, and I'm asking you to marry me and I'm scared to death. And you think I don't know what I'm doing, is that it?"

"Maybe you do know, but *I* certainly don't. I thought you didn't want to marry again, ever."

He hesitated. "I didn't. And I remember that you said you would never marry because of your newspaper."

"I did say that, yes. And I meant it."

"Then has something changed?"

"Nothing has changed for me, Cole. I still can't bear the thought of losing control over the *Sentinel*, but that doesn't mean…" Her eyes flooded with tears. "That d-doesn't mean I don't care for you." She buried her face against his neck and he felt her body tremble.

He let out another groan. "Jess, I need to stop thinking about all this."

"I can't stop thinking about it. Cole, listen. If I cut you loose, so to speak, you could find someone else, someone who wouldn't hesitate to be your wife."

"I don't want anyone else."

"Neither do I, really."

"So…" He pressed his mouth against her hair. "That leaves us with each other."

She nodded slowly. "You know, when you think about it, it's a matter of trust."

"Damn right. You have to trust me not to usurp control over your family newspaper. And I have to trust you—" he gave a halfhearted laugh "—not to die and break my heart."

"Oh, Cole," she whispered. "I would never do that."

He was quiet for a long minute, idly combing his fingers through her long, dark hair. "My wife didn't die accidentally, Jess. She was killed."

"Oh, yes, I remember."

He tightened his arms around her. "You came close, too, the night your office was firebombed."

"Oh," she said again. "I see now."

He chuckled softly. "I'd still marry you. I'll just have to pray a lot."

"I—I guess I'm the one who's not ready to take the risk."

He sighed. "Guess not." He felt as if he were butting up against an oak tree. She wouldn't budge, and he couldn't get her to bend. That meant he had no choice.

Damn. It was like opening a handsomely bound book to find all the pages had been ripped out. There would never be a story written on them. He pressed his lips into her hair. He loved her. And she loved him; at least she said she did.

But maybe not enough.

Chapter Twenty-Five

On Tuesday morning a week later, Jess noticed that Eli was acting a little peculiar. More than a little, in fact. He sat hunched oddly over his type stick, his head down so low his nose almost brushed the font case. Every so often a strange sound hung on the air, a high sort of whine.

"Eli, are you wheezing?"

"Not me, by cracky. Ain't never wheezed in my life."

There, she heard it again. "What *is* that noise?"

The old man lifted his head a fraction of an inch. "What noise?"

"*That* noise. Don't you hear it?"

"Nope." He ducked his head and rattled a handful of type fonts onto his table. Jess shrugged, picked up her pencil and idly studied Eli while she gathered her thoughts for the editorial she planned on planting spring flowers.

All at once she noted that Eli was keeping one hand in his vest pocket. Had he injured it? Maybe gotten it caught in the lawn mower Ilsa Rowell kept on her back porch? She knew Eli liked to help out at the boardinghouse; maybe he'd burned a finger baking a batch of his oatmeal cookies.

Or maybe not. "Eli, what do you have in your pocket?"

"N-nuthin', Jess."

"Eli?"

The old man ducked his head even farther, patted his vest pocket and then shamefacedly drew forth a tiny ball of orange fluff and set it next to his type stick.

A kitten! Jess shot to her feet. "Oh, the darling little thing!"

Eli tried not to grin. "Ya don't mind?"

"Oh, Eli, it's so sweet. Of course I don't mind. I adore kittens. Especially orange ones. Mama used to have a big orange mama cat, and when it curled up on the settee it looked just like a bowl of orange sherbet."

"Yeah, it's cute, ain't it?" He waggled his forefinger to catch the kitten's attention, and the animal followed it around and around on the table top. "Spins jest like one of them whirlin' dervishes."

Jess's heart lifted. After the past few weeks of chasing after stories that didn't amount to anything newsworthy, and trying *not* to chase after Cole, she needed a distraction. "That's just what we'll call him, Eli. Dervish."

"Um, well, hate to tell ya this, Jess, but this here cute little critter ain't a 'him.' It's a 'her.'"

"Oh. It doesn't matter. 'Dervish' is a neutral name."

Eli studiously smoothed his gnarled hand over the animal's thick orange fur. "Hate to tell ya somethin' else, Jess."

"Oh? What's that?"

He avoided her eyes. "Dervish done peed in my vest pocket."

Within two days, Dervish had made herself at home in the *Sentinel* office. Eli fed her scraps of bacon and fried eggs from Ilsa's breakfast table, and during the day the kitten scampered about, intoxicated with the interesting playthings she found. A crumpled piece of notepaper. Eli's shoelaces. The buttons on Jessamine's shirtwaists, which the animal batted at while perched on her desk. At night Dervish slept at the foot of Jess's bed.

The next week was the first week of spring, and Jess kept herself busy reporting on the happenings around Smoke River. Jericho Silver again traveled to Portland to take his law examination, and this time he passed it. When he returned, Maddie invited Jess and Cole over for a celebration, complete with champagne and a burnt-sugar cake from Uncle Charlie's Bakery.

The following Monday Jericho presided at the trials of Conway Arbuckle on the charge of attempted murder for his role in firebombing the *Sentinel* office and Jim Trautner on the charge of kidnapping Cole.

The proceedings took place as the first daffodils began to bloom in gardens all over town, including, Jess noted with distaste, the run-down two-story frame house belonging to that disreputable woman, Lucy, the one Rosie Greywolf referred to as Arbuckle's "other wife."

Juries found both Arbuckle and Trautner guilty, and Sheriff Anderson Rivera escorted the two men to the state prison east of Portland. That same day, Rosie Greywolf visited the *Sentinel* office.

When the Indian woman spied Dervish, her dark eyebrows drew together. "Keep inside," she warned. "Coyotes close to town."

"Thank you for the warning, Rosie."

"Also bring news," Rosie said. "For newspaper."

"Oh?" Rosie was an invaluable source of news around town, a source that Cole did not have access to. "What have you heard?"

"Hear nothing," came the terse reply. "But Rosie *see* much."

Jess picked up a pencil and her notepad. "Tell me."

The older woman's black eyes snapped with

amusement. "First Mrs. Coffee Man leave town. And then Second Mrs. leave town, also."

"Really?"

"Together."

"You mean…why, they can't possibly be friends."

"Not friends, maybe, but go same place. On same day. On same train."

Jess put her pencil down. "How do you know this?"

The Indian woman licked her lips. "I watch. Good story, eh?"

So, Mrs. Arbuckle and Lucy Whatsername, Arbuckle's fancy woman, had joined forces, so to speak. Conway Arbuckle was on his way to prison, and this new bit of information would be a juicy piece of news for the next issue of the *Sentinel*.

She could hardly wait to see Cole's face when he read it.

The next afternoon Rosie Greywolf appeared in Cole's newspaper office.

"Rosie," Cole greeted the Indian woman. "What can I do for you?"

"You should know this thing," she began.

Cole waited. "What should I know?"

"About house. Coffee Man's other wife's house."

"You mean Lucy Gaynor's place? What about it?"

"Empty now," Rosie pronounced.

"Ye-es." Again he waited.

Rosie pinned him with sharp black eyes. "Needs fix-up."

"Ah."

The woman peered up at him as if doubting he had even half a brain. "You fix up."

"Me! Why? I don't own the place."

"Buy, maybe. Very cheap."

"Rosie, I live upstairs here. I don't need a house."

"You need," she persisted. Her gaze swung across the street to the *Sentinel* office and back to Cole. "Come summer," she pronounced.

His collar felt too tight. "Yeah? What about summer?"

Rosie blew out a long-suffering breath, and all at once Cole understood. Rosie Greywolf thought he'd need a bigger place to live come summer because...

Jumping jennies! Because the Indian woman expected that he and Jess...

"Rosie, what makes you think Miss Lassiter and I...?"

The woman huffed in exasperation and rolled her eyes. "Thought you smart, Newsman," she said. Then she spun on her moccasins and glided out the door.

I'll be damned. Did Rosie know something he didn't?

That afternoon he coerced Jess into going for a walk, ostensibly to enjoy the flower gardens in bloom.

"Oh, look," she exclaimed. "Sweet peas! See? On that trellis."

"Yeah. Kinda pretty."

They made their way up one street and down another while Jess oohed and aahed over pansies and roses and something called Love in a Mist. By the time they reached Lucy's abandoned house on Maple Street, Cole was having doubts as big as boulders.

The place was more than run-down; it needed paint and new porch planks and God knew what else. Besides, what made him think Jess would even give the house a second glance?

But her reaction made him laugh. "Oh, Cole, look! That's the house that belonged to that woman, Lucy. Arbuckle's fancy lady."

Apparently most women liked seeing a well-designed house, no matter who the previous owner had been. Then again, Jess wasn't most women.

"What a handsome front porch. See? It runs all across the front of the house and wraps around the corner."

"Uh-huh."

"But—" she tsked "—just look at that poor neglected garden. The roses need pruning, and it looks like no one's ever watered the petunias."

"The place has been vacant for a month. Want to see the inside?"

At her first step past the unlocked front door, Jess stopped short and gazed around. "My, it is lovely, isn't it? I was so intent on finding Arbuckle that day I paid no attention to the interior."

"Looks pretty dusty to me."

"But look at the bones," she said.

"Bones? What are bones?"

"You know, the structure. Look! The windows are nice and large and there's a handsome brick fireplace in the front parlor." She darted on into the dining room.

"Wainscoting!" she enthused. "And another fireplace."

She stepped into the kitchen and stopped short. "Oh." Her voice fell. "These walls are filthy, and the stove is a disaster, all that grease and soot."

"Yeah, it's a mess, all right."

"But…" She stood tapping one finger against her chin. "One must always look beneath the surface of things."

She turned to him, her gray-green eyes shining like two pieces of polished jade. "I want to see the upstairs."

Before he could stop her, she tore up the wooden staircase at the end of the front hall, and Cole heard her delighted squeal.

"There are two—no, three bedrooms," she called. "And a big sitting room, and they *all* have fireplaces. Arbuckle must have made millions on his coffee to maintain a place like this for his mistress, in addition to a suite of rooms at the hotel for his wife."

"I try never to drink his brand of coffee," Cole muttered.

He started up the stairs just as Jess came back down. "Every bedroom up there has lovely tall windows. I wonder what that woman, Lucy, did with all these rooms."

"Entertained, maybe?"

"Ha! Entertained who? Nobody respectable would ever call on her, would they?"

"Dunno. I think her callers might not have been the most respectable types. I've never known such a woman well."

Her eyes narrowed. "What do you mean, 'well'?"

"I mean well enough to call on her. Or ask her what she did with a big old rambling house like this."

"It is rambling, isn't it?" She worried her bottom lip. "That's what I like about it. It has, well, possibilities."

"Possibilities," he repeated.

Her face took on a glow he'd never seen before. "Yes, possibilities. For a family, you know? A big family, to fill all those bedrooms. It reminds me—"

She broke off.

"Reminds you of what, Jess?" He waited, trying to calm the flock of sparrows that just winged their way into his belly.

"Oh," she said, her eyes growing misty. "It reminds me of our house in the East, before Mama died. Lace curtains everywhere, and wallpaper, beautiful wallpaper. Blue flowers in some rooms, and yellow stripes in the dining room. I always liked wallpaper," she said wistfully. "I still miss that house."

He took her hand. "There's a yard out back. Big garden space. You want to see it?"

"N-no." Her eyes looked shiny.

Damn, he didn't want to upset her. He just wanted to show her the empty house, see if she liked it. He slipped an arm around her shoulders. "Come on, Jess. It's not worth crying about. Let's go on over to the hotel and have some coff—um, tea."

She nodded and walked out the front door. Then, in a gesture that twisted his heart, she caught his free hand and held on tight.

Chapter Twenty-Six

Jess ripped open the crisp white envelope and spread the single sheet on her desk.

Dear Miss Lassiter,

I am pleased to inform you that your news story of April eighteenth concerning the ongoing campaigns of General George C. Custer has garnered the favorable attention of the Association of Oregon Journalists. Consequently, the Association takes pleasure in issuing this invitation to publish a monthly guest column in the Portland Oregonian.

We sincerely hope you will accept.

Very truly yours,

Rufus M. Bidwell

Editor in Chief,

Portland Oregonian

She sucked in her breath, her pencil halfway to its usual place between her teeth. Wonder of wonders! She'd written a really good story. A really, really good story.

She'd gotten the idea from Rosie Greywolf, who had glided into her office one sunshiny morning and poked a worn finger at an article Jess had published in her Saturday edition about the latest exploits of George Custer in Colorado Territory.

"You listen," Rosie had murmured. "White man does not like Indian man. Will be big trouble soon."

"What kind of trouble, Rosie?"

"You heard of place called Sand Creek?"

Jess could not meet the woman's unblinking gaze. "Yes, I read about it in a Portland newspaper. A massacre, it said."

"Will happen again. Indian will take revenge for army killing many women. Many children."

"Rosie, how do you know this?"

"I am Cheyenne. My mother, my brothers were at Sand Creek."

When Jess wrote her next story about Custer's Indian raids, she had remembered Rosie's words about the massacre at Sand Creek.

The flutters in her belly turned into a herd of horses and then into a thundering freight train. She was learning to be a really good journalist! Miles would be proud of her. *Papa would be proud of me.*

Her breath stopped. She'd always heard that success was intoxicating. She'd never believed it, but now she knew it was true. It seeped into one's blood, like opium, and she never wanted it to stop. At that moment she knew she would never, never be able to give up her newspaper career.

Not only that, but she knew she did not want to share it, not even with someone she thought of as highly as she did Cole Sanders.

But oh! She couldn't wait to tell him about her letter from Rufus Bidwell.

She sped across the street to the *Lark* office, congratulating herself on uncovering the news before her competition. She couldn't wait to tell Cole her discovery.

Taking a deep breath, she burst through the door of his office and came to a dead stop.

"Where is he?" she asked a startled Noralee.

The girl glanced up from the type stick on the table before her. "He went out real early, Miss Jessamine."

"Do you know where he went?"

Noralee ducked her head. "He said he was going to Gillette Springs. Took that Arabian horse of his and rode off first thing this morning."

Jessamine studied the girl. "Why Gillette Springs?"

"Dunno, ma'am. He said it was important."

Important? What could be so important that Cole would dash off on a Saturday morning? A news story. That was it! She clenched her teeth. One she hadn't heard about.

Yet.

But…she smiled inwardly. She knew something that was happening in town that Cole *didn't* know. Something very interesting.

He did not return to town until long past suppertime, and when Jess saw him stride up the boardwalk and disappear into the *Lark* office, she stuffed her pencil and notepad into a desk drawer and flew across the street.

"Cole, you'll never guess what?"

His dark eyebrows rose. "Okay, I give up. What?"

"You remember that house, the one on Maple Street?"

"Yeah," he said, his voice wary. "Lucy Gaynor's old place. What about it?"

"Ike Bruhn is fixing it up! He's repairing the floor in the kitchen, and just yesterday he installed a brand-new stove, a beautiful new Windsor with a double oven and a special reservoir for hot water."

"You don't say." His tone sounded weary. "Never thought you'd get so excited about something as domestic as a stove."

"And a porcelain bathtub upstairs," she added. "A big one."

"You don't say," he repeated.

Why was he not as curious about these events as she was? She was positive there was a news story in all this; she could practically smell it.

"Cole, who owns that house?"

"Lucy Gaynor owned it. Maybe she still does."

"But Lucy is gone. She and Mrs. Arbuckle moved to Portland after the trial, remember? We both wrote a story about it."

"Maybe she's planning to return."

Jess stared at him. He met her gaze, his mouth quirked. "That'd be a first, don't you think, Jess? Could be she wants to open a—"

"Oh!" Her eyes went wide. "Wouldn't *that* be a story?"

He shook his head tiredly. "I wouldn't go off half-cocked about it if I were you."

"Ooh, the clues make my fingers positively itch!"

Cole suppressed a grin. "If you can contain yourself, would you care to take supper with me?"

"Could we walk by Lucy's house on the way?"

He laughed. "Sure. Gotta keep an eye on those roses in the front yard you said needed pruning."

She shot him a withering look. "Roses!" She sniffed. "Roses are not the least bit newsworthy. Come on, let's go see the house."

Cole let her drag him along Maple Street, but the closer they drew to the place, the harder he worked to keep pace with her.

"Look!" She pulled him to a halt at the front gate.

"There's a brand-new front door, with colored glass insets!"

"Yep, I see 'em."

"And the walkway up to the porch is wider than I remember. Whoever is paying for all this must be rich."

"Have you asked Ike who hired him?"

"Of course."

"And?"

"Ike just grins. That man is closemouthed as a clam."

She danced up the porch steps and swept through the front door, and he heard her cry of surprise. "Cole! There's new wallpaper in the dining room. *Yellow* wallpaper."

"You approve?"

"Oh, yes. Whoever is doing this has exquisite taste, don't you think?"

"I wouldn't know, Jess. I don't know a thing about stoves or wallpaper or…"

"Bathtubs," she supplied. "Come upstairs." She darted up the staircase. Cole sauntered up after her, drew her away from the shiny white porcelain tub and planted a kiss on her flushed cheek. "Getting hungry?"

"No. Yes. No! I want to see more of the house."

"No, you don't. You want to come to supper with me." He snaked his arm across her waist and propelled her back down the stairs, out the front door and along the street toward the restaurant.

All through her chicken croquettes and strawberry shortcake, Jess talked on about the house on Maple Street. Cole worked his way through his rare steak and crispy fried potatoes and apple pie and just listened.

At the door of the *Sentinel* office, he drew her into the shadows and kissed her thoroughly. It sure was hard to talk himself out of taking her upstairs, but she was so wound up with her new discovery he figured she'd rather chatter than kiss him.

He forced himself to walk back across the street to his room above the *Lark* office, and even though he wouldn't be with Jess tonight, he found it impossible to stop smiling.

Chapter Twenty-Seven

A weeping Noralee burst through the door of Jess's office and flung herself into Eli's arms. "Oh, Eli," she sobbed. "It's just awful!"

"Whoa, whoa, honey-girl. What's the problem?"

"It's h-him," she choked out.

"Him? Who's 'him'?"

"Sheriff R-Rivera."

"Why, what's he done, huh?"

Noralee turned her flushed face into his chest and wailed. Over the girl's head, Eli caught Jess's gaze and raised his bushy salt-and-pepper eyebrows in a question. Jess shook her head and silently mouthed, *I don't know.*

Eli patted the girl's shoulder. "All right, now, you tell old Eli all about it, why don'cha? Come on, now, talk to me."

Noralee lifted her head and swiped her palm over her brimming eyes. "Well, I—I baked some chocolate walnut cookies and t-took a quart jar of my special lemonade over to the sheriff's office, and he…he…"

"Mmm-hmm?" Eli murmured. "What'd he do?"

"Nothing!"

"Nuthin', huh?"

"Well, not 'nothing' exactly."

"Well, what, exactly, Norah girl? Did he say thanks?"

"Uh-huh, he did."

"Well, that ain't 'nuthin',' honey. Didja say you're welcome?"

"Y-yes. But he didn't eat my cookies, an' he didn't drink any of my lemonade, not one drop. And I put extra sugar in it and everything."

Eli frowned. "When was all this?"

"Just this morning, Eli."

"What time wouldja say?"

"Around seven o'clock. Right after I finished breakfast."

Jess let out a whoop. "Noralee, he probably wasn't hungry right after breakfast."

"Oh. Miss Jessamine, I never thought of that."

"Well, what *did* he do, huh?" Eli pursued. "Besides sayin' thank you, that is?"

Noralee blew her nose on the red bandanna Eli pressed into her hand. "H-he just patted the top of my head like I was five years old an' went back to readin' the newspaper."

"The *Lark* or the *Sent*—?" Jess clapped her hand over her mouth.

"Don't matter, Jess," Eli rasped. "Her little heart's plumb broke."

"I think it was the *S-Sentinel*, Miss Jessamine. Today's Saturday, isn't it?"

"It is indeed, Noralee."

"Say," Eli said. "You met our new kitten yet? Name's Dervish. Softest da—dern cat I ever laid my big bony fingers on. Come on, let's find him. Her."

Noralee giggled. "Oh, Eli, you're pretty silly sometimes."

"And," Jess added softly, "you're pretty smart, too."

Eli sent her a lopsided grin. "Not bad for an ol' Injun fighter like me, huh?"

After a fitful hour of sleep that night, the moon rose and Jessamine jerked bolt upright in bed as a wild thought struck her.

Gillette Springs? Cole had ridden to Gillette Springs? Why? Gillette Springs was the Lane County seat. And that meant something was afoot. She'd bet a dollar it had something to do with that old abandoned house, the one Ike Bruhn was fixing up.

She was out of bed and dressed in three minutes flat, stuffed her derringer in her skirt pocket, pulled on her sturdy boots and a light jacket and slipped downstairs and out the front door. On her way to the livery stable, she glanced up at the *Lark*'s darkened second-story window. Cole was not awake.

Good.

Inside the stable, she persuaded a sleepy Mose Daniels to saddle a mare for her.

"Where ya goin' at this hour, Miss Jessamine? T'ain't safe."

"I will be perfectly all right, Mose. And don't tell Cole Sanders about it. Promise?"

"But, ma'am, s'cuse me for sayin' so, but y'all cain't ride dressed thataway, in a skirt an' all!"

"I can, and I will," she replied with steel in her voice. Nothing was going to keep her from uncovering whatever news story was happening in Gillette Springs before Cole Sanders did.

She hiked up her skirt, clambered into the saddle and was off on the road to Gillette Springs before she could change her mind.

She rode until her backside was so numb she could no longer feel the saddle before she stopped to rest and water her horse and mop her perspiring face with a lace handkerchief. Heavens, even the early-morning sun was brutal, and summer was over two months away. Her vision was growing blurry, but she kept on.

She gulped the last of the canteen of water Mose had insisted she bring with her and walked her tired mare down the main street of Gillette Springs. She tied the horse at the hitching rail in front of the hotel and forced her legs past the café and the dressmaker and the barbershop, crossed the street and dragged herself up the steps of the brick county courthouse.

"Ma'am, we're closing up," the gray-haired clerk announced.

Jess's heart plummeted into her boots. "Oh, please," she gasped. "I've ridden all the way from Smoke River, and I... I..." Her voice cracked. Tears spilled over her lids, and she swiped her palm across her cheeks. "P-please?"

The embarrassed clerk coughed, looked left and right and then nodded his gray head. "I'll make an exception just this once, miss. What is it that's so important?"

Jess didn't turn up for their usual postmortem breakfast, and when Cole stopped at the *Sentinel* office to check on her, Eli looked at him blankly.

"Ya mean she's not with you?"

"No. She didn't turn up for breakfast and I've not seen her all day. Check upstairs, will you, Eli? Maybe she's sick."

"Already did, Cole. She's not there. Bed's not made, either, and that ain't like her."

Cole's gut clenched. Where the hell was she? Had something happened to her? He wheeled toward the door just as Jess staggered in.

She looked half-dead, her skirt caked with dust,

her hair straggling down the back of her neck. "Jess, what the—?"

His breath choked off.

Her green eyes blazed at him like two heated emeralds. "You…you sneak!" She burst into tears and stuffed her fist against her mouth.

Eli lurched off his stool and limped toward her. Cole stared long and hard at the woman he thought he knew.

And in the next instant he knew everything, where she'd been and, more important, what she had discovered. He stepped in close and wrapped both arms around her.

Eli stared at them, alternately frowning and crushing a wrinkled red bandanna in his hands.

"Jess," Cole murmured. "Jess, I did it for you. I wanted it for you."

"You should have t-told me," she sobbed. "I th-thought there was a news story there, and that I'd get it first and then I could s-scoop your newspaper."

"Would somebody tell me what's goin' on?" Eli yelled.

Jessamine sniffed. "He—he's purchased the old Gaynor place, the house on Maple Street."

"And," Cole added, "I hired Ike Bruhn to do some repairs and—"

"And," Jess wailed, "Cole put the deed in my name!"

Eli's jaw dropped.

"And there's y-yellow wallpaper in the dining room," she sobbed.

Cole cleared his throat. "Oh, hell, honey, I thought you'd like that. One of the upstairs bedrooms has blue flowers. You said—"

"I know what I said, Cole Sanders." She lifted her head to glare up at him. "I said I liked blue wallpaper, but I also said I didn't want to—"

"Yeah," he said heavily, "I remember what you said. But I keep thinking that a man sees what he wants to see and what he doesn't want to see, he... doesn't." He waited a beat. "Or a woman," he added softly.

Eli coughed. "If'n you two'll excuse me, I'm goin' down to the Golden Partridge for a whiskey. A double."

With a last look at Jess, the old man stomped out and slammed the door.

Chapter Twenty-Eight

"Jess," Cole asked, "what made you go off to Gillette Springs in the first place?"

She stared at him, her face flushed, her eyes brimming. "I told you, to get a news story. I thought I could solve the mystery about the Gaynor place, why it's being repaired, who really owns it."

"You can still write a story about it, honey. No one has to know I was the one who bought the house and that I put your name on the deed. Or that I'm the one paying Ike Bruhn to make repairs."

She said nothing, just stared at him while big fat tears rolled down her cheeks.

Cole studied her face. "You know, I think that's not what's really important here."

"Not important!" She bristled up like an affronted banty chicken. "I'll have you know, Cole Sanders, that my newspaper, the *Sentinel*, is important to me. It's my whole life. After Miles was killed I swore I would not let him down, that I would not let my father, or my grandfather, down. That I would preserve our family heritage."

"There are more important things than a news story," he said quietly. "Or a newspaper, for that matter."

Jessamine sank onto Eli's stool and dropped her head into her hands. "I'm so tired I can't think anymore. I've been riding since three o'clock this morning."

"It's almost twenty miles to Gillette Springs. I'm surprised you can even walk."

"I'm not sure I *can* walk," she whispered. "Oh, Cole, I feel like such a fool."

"Yeah," he said. "I agree."

Her head came up. "Well! That's not very gallant."

"I'm not feeling gallant. I'm feeling damn annoyed."

"Yes, I expect you are," she said, her voice wobbly. "Why don't you yell at me or something? I'd feel a whole lot better if you did."

"Nope, I'm not gonna yell at you." He plucked her off the stool, pulled her into his arms and pressed her head against his shoulder. "I figure you need a bath and some supper, in that order. I can yell at you later."

"Yes, oh, yes, a bath…what wonderful ideas you have, Cole. Sometimes."

He suppressed a laugh, lifted her into his arms

and took the stairs up to her room two at a time while Jessamine clung to him, her face buried against his neck.

"Got a washbasin?"

She nodded. "Under my bed."

"I'll heat some water on the stove downstairs. He deposited her on the bed, where she instantly curled up into a ball.

"Don't fall asleep," he warned.

"I won't." Her eyelids closed.

He reached under her bed for the basin. "Get your clothes off," he ordered.

Fifteen minutes later, Cole sat beside her, sponging her naked limbs off with warm water, gritting his teeth to keep from kissing the silky skin.

"I've been thinking," he said. "You remember that night at Christmas when we sang the *Messiah*?"

"Mmm-hmm," she murmured.

He smoothed the soft washcloth over her back and moved slowly down to her bottom. "Something happened to us that night. Did you feel it?"

She mmm-hmmed again, and he went on. "We made love that night, and I felt something I'd never felt before. Something swept over the two of us, and you know what? That something was bigger and more important than just you and me individually. Did you feel it?"

"Yes," she said, her voice lazy. "I felt it."

Cole swallowed. "This might sound way too poetic, Jess, but that night I swear I felt my soul touch yours." His hand stilled on the small of her back. "I've felt that same thing every time we've been together like that."

"Oh, Cole," she said, her voice near tears, "it's like that for me, too."

He drew in a lungful of air, looked away from her and then looked back. "Jess, I'm going to tell you something. Maybe you know this already, but I'm going to tell you anyway. You are headstrong, and brave, and pigheaded, and misguided. And I love you."

As he spoke he dried her skin with a towel he'd warmed on the stove and then he touched one hand to her shoulder. "You want me to bring some supper from the restaurant?"

"No. I'll get dressed. I want to sit across the table from you when I apologize."

"And talk," he growled. "We need to talk."

"Yes," she breathed. "And talk."

Rita set the platters of steak and potatoes down in front of them, and Jess smiled for the first time in twenty-four hours. "I am positively ravenous!" She snatched up her fork, then immediately laid it down again. "Cole?"

"Yeah?"

"I do like the yellow wallpaper in the dining room."

"That's good." He concentrated on cutting into his steak, but his hand started to shake.

"And the blue flowers in the bedroom," she added. "Could we make that room our master bedroom?"

His fork clattered onto the china platter. "What? What did you say?"

"I asked if we could—"

"I heard that part. What I didn't grasp was the 'our' part. As in 'our' bedroom."

"Oh. Well, that's not hard to figure out." She gave up on the steak and dug a spoon into her strawberry shortcake. "I…um… Oh, Cole, it is so hard to apologize. I guess that is part of being pigheaded."

"I guess," he said, his voice quiet. "Keep trying."

She settled her dessert spoon in the empty shortcake bowl, picked it up again and twirled it between her thumb and forefinger.

"You are right," she said, her voice quiet. "There are more important things than a news story, or a newspaper. I guess I haven't been seeing things too clearly."

"Go on."

"Remember the motto printed on your masthead, the one you adopted for your newspaper? 'The truth shall make you free'?"

"Yeah, what about it?"

She leaned toward him and lowered her voice. "Well, um, while I was bouncing around on that saddle on the way to Gillette Springs, I realized that, um, well, maybe for me, the truth is something in myself that I had to face up to."

His knife hand slipped sideways. "God, what else did you figure out?"

"Pride is one of the seven deadly sins, isn't it? I think there are more than seven sins, at least for me. One additional sin might be distrust."

"That's a good sin, too," Cole agreed. "What was it you didn't want to face?" He held his breath.

She answered slowly and dropped her voice to a murmur. "I was willing to trust you with my body and my heart. But…" She pressed her lips together, swallowed hard, and met his eyes. "I wasn't willing to trust you with my newspaper."

"I don't want your newspaper, Jess. I want your heart. And…" He captured her hand, lifted away her spoon and brought her fingers to his lips. "Right now, tonight, I want your body."

Chapter Twenty-Nine

Cole glanced up as the front door of the *Lark* office swung open. Billy Rowell sneaked inside, furtively glanced around and then tiptoed as quietly as he could over to Noralee's typesetting table.

She had not yet arrived, but from Billy's secretive motions, Cole figured the kid already knew that. Quickly Billy withdrew a single yellow rose from inside his blue chambray shirt and laid it beside Noralee's type stick.

He and Cole exchanged a long look. "Ye're not gonna tell on me, are ya?" Billy whispered.

Without speaking, Cole sketched a large cross over his chest and tried hard not to grin. He'd bet Billy would like Noralee's lemonade just fine. In fact, he'd bet Noralee would take one look at that yellow rose and be head over heels in love again.

Billy saluted and disappeared out the door.

Cole laid his pencil down beside the notepad on his desk. And right then and there he made a decision.

Jessamine swung along the boardwalk, feeling the warm spring sunshine on her face and inhaling the heady sweet scent of blooming lilacs. This morning's copy of Cole's *Lark* newspaper was folded under her arm.

Verena Forester passed her going the opposite direction. "Good morning," the dressmaker said in a cheery voice as she swept on.

Jess halted in her tracks. How odd. Verena Forester was never cheery in the morning. Verena was never cheery at any time of day.

Whitey Poletti stopped sweeping the sidewalk in front of his barbershop and gave her a grin, then bent his pudgy frame into a low bow. "Miss Jessamine."

Hmm. Whitey had never smiled at her this early in the morning before; was the man getting addled? She marched on past the mercantile, and all at once Noralee Ness rushed out and threw her thin arms around Jessamine's waist.

"Heavens!" Jess exclaimed. "What is that for? You already have a job at the *Lark*."

Noralee's brown eyes shone with unshed tears. "Oh, Miss Jessamine, I'm so happy!"

Good Lord, surely Anderson Rivera had not proposed marriage?

She swept into the restaurant and found her way

to her usual table in the corner. Rita beamed at her and hurried over with a pot of her favorite tea.

She poured her cup full and stirred in a double spoonful of sugar and then began to notice Rita's sidelong glances. The waitress seemed overly smiley this morning. In fact, everyone seemed unusually smiley this morning.

Now that she thought about it, even Eli had acted strange, as if he couldn't stop grinning over some private joke.

Rita approached, nervously twiddling her pencil.

"Rita, what is the matter with everyone this morning?"

The waitress's eyes crinkled at the corners. "You see this morning's *Lark* yet, Miss Jessamine?"

"Why, no. Mr. Sanders and I usually read over each other's newspapers together and then we critique them over breakfast. He should be here any minute."

"I think you'd better read today's *Lark* before he gets here," the waitress murmured.

"Oh? Why is that?"

Rita sidled away without answering, and Jessamine frowned. Oh, very well, she would read it. She unfolded the Friday edition of Cole's newspaper, spread it across the dining table and choked on her tea.

Emblazoned across the front page, in seventy-two-point boldface type, the single headline leaped out at her.

JESSAMINE LASSITER—
WILL YOU MARRY ME?

Speechless, she sat staring at the words until her eyes burned.

Rita began dabbing tears off her cheeks with the hem of her ruffled apron.

And then Cole walked in.

He shouldered his way past a gaggle of restaurant employees reaching out to shake his hand and made his way to where she sat.

Jessamine half rose from her chair.

"Well?" he breathed, glancing at the page spread across the table. "Too many *m*'s?"

She gave a choked laugh and flung her arms about his neck.

"Too many *s*'s," she whispered," kissing his chin. "As in *Yes. Yes! Yes.*"

"Oh, thank God," he breathed. "I don't have any more seventy-two-point type."

Shortly afterward the *Smoke River Sentinel* and the *Lane County Lark* printed identical stories on their society pages.

Jessamine Marie Lassiter and Coleridge Whitney Sanders were joined in marriage on Saturday the fourteenth day of May at the Smoke River Community Church. Mr. Elijah Holst gave the bride away, and Colonel Washington Halliday stood as best man.

Miss Noralee Ness served as flower girl.

The bride wore her mother's wedding gown of ivory silk trimmed with Valenciennes lace and carried a bouquet of yellow roses.

Judge Jericho Silver officiated at the ceremony, which was followed by a reception at Rose Cottage, hosted by Rooney and Sarah Rose Cloudman. Champagne and a burnt-sugar wedding cake from Uncle Charlie's Bakery were enjoyed by over fifty guests.

Following a brief honeymoon in Portland, the couple will reside at 209 Maple Street.

In accordance with the wishes of the editors of the *Sentinel* and the *Lark*, both newspapers will resume publication as usual, with no disruption in service.

* * * * *

REQUEST YOUR FREE BOOKS!

⊕ HARLEQUIN®

ℋISTORICAL

Where love is timeless

2 FREE NOVELS PLUS 2 **FREE GIFTS!**

YES! Please send me 2 FREE Harlequin® Historical novels and my 2 FREE gifts (gifts are worth about $10). After receiving them, if I don't wish to receive any more books, I can return the shipping statement marked "cancel." If I don't cancel, I will receive 6 brand-new novels every month and be billed just $5.69 per book in the U.S. or $5.99 per book in Canada. That's a savings of at least 12% off the cover price! It's quite a bargain! Shipping and handling is just 50¢ per book in the U.S. and 75¢ per book in Canada.* I understand that accepting the 2 free books and gifts places me under no obligation to buy anything. I can always return a shipment and cancel at any time. Even if I never buy another book, the two free books and gifts are mine to keep forever.

246/349 HDN GH2Z

Name	(PLEASE PRINT)	
Address		Apt. #
City	State/Prov.	Zip/Postal Code

Signature (if under 18, a parent or guardian must sign)

Mail to the **Reader Service:**
IN U.S.A.: P.O. Box 1867, Buffalo, NY 14240-1867
IN CANADA: P.O. Box 609, Fort Erie, Ontario L2A 5X3

Want to try two free books from another line?
Call 1-800-873-8635 or visit www.ReaderService.com.

* Terms and prices subject to change without notice. Prices do not include applicable taxes. Sales tax applicable in N.Y. Canadian residents will be charged applicable taxes. Offer not valid in Quebec. This offer is limited to one order per household. Not valid for current subscribers to Harlequin Historical books. All orders subject to credit approval. Credit or debit balances in a customer's account(s) may be offset by any other outstanding balance owed by or to the customer. Please allow 4 to 6 weeks for delivery. Offer available while quantities last.

Your Privacy—The Reader Service is committed to protecting your privacy. Our Privacy Policy is available online at www.ReaderService.com or upon request from the Reader Service.

We make a portion of our mailing list available to reputable third parties that offer products we believe may interest you. If you prefer that we not exchange your name with third parties, or if you wish to clarify or modify your communication preferences, please visit us at www.ReaderService.com/consumerschoice or write to us at Reader Service Preference Service, P.O. Box 9062, Buffalo, NY 14240-9062. Include your complete name and address.

SPECIAL EXCERPT FROM

HARLEQUIN®

HISTORICAL

*Runaway heiress Lorna Bradford must reach
California to claim her fortune, but when she's rescued
from robbers by fierce Cheyenne warrior Black Horse,
she's forced to remain under his protection!*

Read on for a sneak preview of
HER CHEYENNE WARRIOR, by
Lauri Robinson.

"Lie down, Poeso. Your day was long. You are tired."

Her glance was weary, and wary, and she shook her head.

"Black Horse protect you." Gesturing toward the doorway, he said, "No one will enter my lodge."

Still shaking her head, she whispered, "Who will protect me from you?"

Another whisper of understanding angered him, turned his insides dark. A man had hurt her. A bad man in a bad way.

"Black Horse protect you from all." He backed away and then moved across the lodge to repair his bed. Afterward he retrieved his pouch from where it hung on a lodge pole and pulled out the gun. Trust had to be mutual or it was nothing.

"Here is your gun, Poeso," he said, holding it out for her to take.

Her eyes were big and full of surprise, and her hand shook as she reached for the little pistol.

He laid it in her palm and wrapped both of his hands around hers. "I trust you, Poeso. You trust Black Horse."

She looked from him to their hands and back up at his face. "Are the bullets still in it?"

Her voice was soft, and the words cracked, but he understood she had to say them. "Yes." Letting go of her hands, he pointed to the buffalo hides. "Go to bed, Poeso, you are safe."

He waited, hoping his heart was right, that he could trust her, and then watched her scoot onto the furs. She kept the gun clutched near her chest, even after lying down on her side.

Black Horse moved to his bed. This might become a sleepless night. He had never slept next to a woman holding a gun. Once stretched out on his back, he listened for any movement she might make.

"What does *poeso* mean?" she asked quietly.

"Cat."

"Why do you call me that?"

"Because that is what you remind me of. The sleek mountain lions that roam the hills."

"Is that bad?"

"*Hova'ahane,*" he answered. "*Epeva'e.*"

"*Epeva'e,*" she repeated. "It is good?"

"*Heehe'e,*" he said. "It is good."

Don't miss
HER CHEYENNE WARRIOR by Lauri Robinson,
available June 2016 wherever
Harlequin® Historical books and ebooks are sold.

www.Harlequin.com

Reading Has Its Rewards

Earn **FREE BOOKS!**

Register at **Harlequin My Rewards** and submit your Harlequin purchases from wherever you shop to earn points for free books and other exclusive rewards.

Plus submit your purchases from now till May 30th for a chance to win a $500 Visa Card*.

Visit **HarlequinMyRewards.com** today

MYR16R1